# Goosebumps
# WANTED
# THE HAUNTED MASK

# R.L. STINE

SCHOLASTIC PRESS/New York

# GOOSEBUMPS®
## NOW WITH BONUS FEATURES!

NIGHT OF THE LIVING DUMMY

DEEP TROUBLE

MONSTER BLOOD

THE HAUNTED MASK

ONE DAY AT HORRORLAND

THE CURSE OF THE MUMMY'S TOMB

BE CAREFUL WHAT YOU WISH FOR

SAY CHEESE AND DIE!

THE HORROR AT CAMP JELLYJAM

HOW I GOT MY SHRUNKEN HEAD

THE WEREWOLF OF FEVER SWAMP

A NIGHT IN TERROR TOWER

WELCOME TO DEAD HOUSE

WELCOME TO CAMP NIGHTMARE

GHOST BEACH

THE SCARECROW WALKS AT MIDNIGHT

YOU CAN'T SCARE ME!

RETURN OF THE MUMMY

REVENGE OF THE LAWN GNOMES

PHANTOM OF THE AUDITORIUM

VAMPIRE BREATH

STAY OUT OF THE BASEMENT

GET MORE GOOSEBUMPS® ON DVD!
FROM FOX HOME ENTERTAINMENT

Ride for your life!

Goosebumps HorrorLand™ the video game
from Scholastic Interactive

GET GOOSEBUMPS PHOTOSHOCK FOR YOUR
iPhone™ OR iPod touch®

Library of Congress Cataloging-in-Publication Data

Stine, R. L.
Goosebumps wanted : the haunted mask / by R.L. Stine. — 1st ed.
p. cm.
Summary: When she discovers an evil mask at the bottom of a trunk and puts it on, LuAnn's Halloween turns into a real nightmare because only an act of unbelievable kindness can remove it.
ISBN 978-0-545-41793-8
1. Masks — Juvenile fiction. 2. Halloween — Juvenile fiction. 3. Horror tales. [1. Horror stories. 2. Masks — Fiction. 3. Halloween — Fiction.]
I. Title. II. Title: Haunted mask.
PZ7.S86037Gor 2012
813.54 — dc23
2012000151

Goosebumps book series created by Parachute Press, Inc.
Copyright © 2012 by Scholastic Inc.

12  11  10  9  8  7  6  5  4  3  2  1          12  13  14  15  16/0

Printed in the U.S.A.                                                23
First printing, July 2012

# WANTED

# PART ONE:

# THE HAUNTED MASK

# 1

The bell over the shop door jingled. The door swung open, and a woman and a little girl entered. Their eyes darted over the shelves and display cases of masks.

William lowered his feather duster and turned to the front of his store. He had been gently dusting the shelf of delicate princess masks. They were precious, and he dusted them every day.

All of his masks were precious to him. He cared for them as if they were his children.

As the woman and girl approached, Hansel lifted his big head and sniffed the air. The old

German shepherd didn't like to have his nap interrupted. But William was always happy to see customers. People he could share his beloved masks with.

"Welcome," he said. His voice was still young and crisp, despite his seventy years. His mustache was white, as was his wavy hair, parted in the middle. But his eyes were sharp, and he had the energy of a much younger man.

He brushed back the black cape he wore to give himself a look of mystery and set down the feather duster. "Welcome to William's Mask Emporium." He smiled at the little girl, who was dark haired and pretty. She wore a pink pleated skirt and a matching pink sweater. "Did you come to buy a mask?"

"Olivia is going to a costume party," her mother said. "We heard you have the best mask store in town."

William bowed his head. "I think it's the best. It's certainly the oldest. The store has been in my family for three generations."

Olivia was staring at a round pig mask in the first display case. The color matched her skirt and sweater. "Is that a real pig head?" Her voice trembled.

William chuckled. "Of course not. It's made of rubber. Do you like it, Olivia? I made it myself."

4

Olivia shook her head. "No, I don't want to be a pig."

Her mother stepped up to the line of princess masks. "These are pretty, Olivia. Come take a look."

Olivia had to step around the dog, who was sprawled on his side, his legs stretching over the narrow aisle. "What's your dog's name?"

"Hansel," William told her. "He's a good dog. But he isn't interested in masks, so he sleeps all day." William handed her a princess mask. "Try this one. It goes well with your dark hair."

He turned to her mother. "The masks in this case are all handmade. I hope you like my craftsmanship."

"It's nice to see someone who takes so much pride in his work," she replied.

Olivia tried on four princess masks. Then they bought the first one that William had handed her. William wrapped it carefully in brown paper. "Enjoy the party," he called after them. The bell jangled as they left.

William locked the cash register. He dimmed the lights. "Come on, Hansel. Stand up. It's time to go home."

Hansel lifted his head but didn't move. William wrapped his hands around the dog's middle and hoisted him to his feet. "It's a short walk home,

5

dog. You can go back to sleep as soon as we get there."

He led the big dog outside and locked the shop door. The late afternoon was dark, with low storm clouds overhead. Sheets of fog greeted him as he started to walk.

William shivered and pulled the black cape tighter around his slender frame. He took long strides. Hansel had to trot to keep up with him.

"Such a thick fog," he said to the dog. "I can barely see where I am going. You are lucky to have four legs. Makes it easier to walk."

The fog billowed like a heavy curtain. The street was silent.

They had walked only a few blocks when the dog suddenly stopped. A low growl escaped Hansel's throat. William saw the fur on his back stand straight up.

He lowered a hand to Hansel's head. "What is it, boy? What is frightening you?"

The dog uttered another growl, fiercer than the first.

William heard the click of footsteps behind him. He turned but could see only a pulsing wall of white fog.

The dog growled. The footsteps stopped.

"Who's there?" William called. "Who is it?"

No answer.

One hand on the dog's head, William listened hard. But all he could hear was the whistle of the wind as it swirled the waves of fog.

"No one there, Hansel." But the dog remained tense.

William started to walk again. And once more, he heard the clicking footsteps close behind him. Hansel growled again.

William spun around again. "Is anyone there? I can't see you in this fog."

Silence.

A shiver of fear ran down the old man's back. "Is anyone there? Please answer."

No reply.

He was happy when he stepped up to the front door of his house, unlocked it, and made his way inside. Hansel shook himself, as if shaking off the fog. William locked the door carefully behind him.

He fed the dog and had a quiet dinner himself. Then he hurried to his workshop, where he spent most nights. Hansel found his usual comfortable spot on the carpet in one corner.

"What shall we work on tonight?" William murmured. "You know, Hansel, I have some new brown fur. I'll make some cute monkey masks to sell in the shop."

William had several plain white masks he had shaped as monkey heads. Tonight he would apply glue over the fronts and attach the fur.

He hummed to himself as he started to work his glue brush over the first mask. Hansel snored quietly in the corner.

They were both interrupted by several loud thuds.

The dog jerked his head up, instantly alert. It took William a few seconds to realize someone was pounding on the front door. Pounding hard.

He set down the glue brush and wiped his hands on a towel.

The pounding on the door grew louder.

"Okay, okay. I'm coming."

William had few visitors. *Who would come out on a cold, foggy night like this?*

He hesitated before opening the door. The heavy pounding had stopped. All he could hear was the rush of wind on the other side.

William gripped the handle and pulled the front door open. He recognized his visitor at once. He gasped. And cried out:

"What are *you* doing here?"

The younger man squinted into the light at William. "Is that any way to greet your brother? Aren't you even going to allow me in?"

Shaking off his surprise, William stepped back to allow his brother to enter. "Randolph, I haven't seen you in years."

"I had to follow you in the fog, William. I didn't even know where my own brother lives."

William frowned. "Last time, our parting was *not* friendly. I'm sure you remember."

"The past is the past," Randolph replied, glancing around the front room. He was taller than William. His hair was still black, as was his mustache. He wore a heavy gray overcoat and carried a black leather bag that looked like a doctor's case.

They both turned as Hansel stepped into the room, growling. The dog had his head lowered, as if preparing to attack.

"I can't believe that creature is still alive." Randolph raised the case in front of him like a shield. "Can you make him stop that ugly snarling?"

"Hansel is a good judge of character," William said quietly. He eyed his brother. *Why has he come here?*

"I told you, William, let the past be the past," Randolph snapped. "We are brothers, after all. The world has changed since we last met. Perhaps I have changed my ways, too."

"Perhaps," William replied. He signaled Hansel to relax.

The dog stopped growling but kept his big brown eyes steady on the visitor.

Randolph set the black case down on the small table where William ate his dinners. He shrugged off the heavy overcoat and draped it over the back of a chair.

William saw that his brother's suit was shabby and worn. One pocket was torn and the shirt cuffs were badly frayed.

*He needs money. He has come to ask me for money.*

"Randolph, what brings you here?"

William's brother rubbed his hands together, warming them. He shivered his shoulders. "Cold out there."

"Yes. Did you come to bring me a weather report?"

Randolph snickered. "You have a sharp tongue, brother. In fact, I came here to help you. I came to help make you famous. Perhaps rich and famous."

William rolled his eyes. "That's a laugh. You came to help *me*? That would be the first time, wouldn't it."

"Times change," Randolph muttered. He moved to the case. He struggled with the latch. "William, you will change your tune when you see what I have brought for you."

William stepped up beside his brother, eyes on the case. He had no reason to trust Randolph. Randolph was a criminal, plain and simple. William believed he had even done time in prison.

Randolph reached deep into the case and pulled out a green-and-blue object. He unfolded it. A mask. Holding it in both hands, he raised the mask in front of him.

William heard a yelp. He turned in time to see the frightened look on Hansel's face. For the second time that night, the dog's fur rose stiff on his back. And uttering pitiful whines, the big dog wheeled around and ran from the room.

Randolph laughed. "Your beast is afraid of masks."

William stared at the mask in his brother's hands. The face was twisted and ugly, covered in bulging warts. A fat blue tongue hung from the mouth. The tongue was also covered in warts. The ears appeared to be dripping with yellow pus.

"It's very ugly," William said. "I want to run away from it, too."

Randolph ignored that comment. He reached into the leather case and pulled out another mask. Another ugly, twisted, wart-pocked face. Then a third one.

This was green and shaped like an insect's head. It had two rows of spiky, pointed teeth and big pointed ears. A demon's face!

"Put them away," William said. "Masks should be beautiful. Delicate. I cannot stand to see such ugliness."

"You don't understand," Randolph insisted. "These will make you famous. Your shop will be known around the world."

William shuddered. He turned his eyes away from the ugly green mask. "You brought these here to sell to me?"

His brother nodded. "I will give you a good price. I . . . I'm a little short of cash. You know how it is. A little needy right now. You can pay me less than these are worth."

"But I don't want them!" William said. "They are too ugly. They will scare the children. I make masks for children, Randolph. I can't have these in my shop."

"Idiot!" Randolph snapped. He tossed the green mask onto the pile of masks on the table. "Don't you see? I haven't brought you ordinary masks. Have you no eyes? These aren't masks!"

"Not masks? Then what are they?" William demanded.

"They are faces. Human faces."

William uttered a loud gasp. He took a step

back from the table. "What are you saying? What do you mean?"

"These faces used to talk and smile," Randolph said. "Look, brother. Look at them." He turned the case upside down and several tumbled to the table. William counted at least a dozen of them.

"But —" William couldn't find words. He realized his heart was beating hard in his chest.

"These are the faces no one wanted," Randolph said, spitting the words in William's face. "Too ugly. Too sick. Too twisted. No one wanted them. No one wanted to see them. They are The Unwanted. The Unwanted Faces of the world."

William stared hard at the pile of faces. Could his brother be telling the truth?

"Take them away, Randolph. I find this very . . . upsetting."

"No." Randolph grabbed William's sleeve. "Go ahead. Touch them. Touch just one. Pick one up."

"No. Please —"

Randolph tugged his brother's hand, pulled it to the table. "Touch one. Go ahead. Do it, coward!"

William swallowed hard. He felt his dinner rise to his throat. He suddenly felt very sick.

"Do it! Touch it!"

William reached for a mask. He smoothed his fingers over its cheek. "Oh, good heavens. Oh, no. Oh, please — no."

Randolph laughed.

William gasped again. He jerked his hand away. "It . . . It's skin. Human skin. And it feels warm."

Randolph nodded, his dark eyes flashing. "I'm telling you the truth, William. Don't you see? If you put these in your shop, people will talk. People will —"

"No!" William cried. "No! Listen to me. I don't know where you got these faces, Randolph. These poor souls. I don't care where you got them. I just want them out of my house. I will not have them in my shop. And I will not have them — or *you* — in my house!"

In his anger, William grabbed the smooth green mask with the pointed ears and the rows of ugly teeth. He intended to jam it back into the leather case. But it seemed to cling to his hand.

He spun it around and studied its ugly, frightening face. "This one —"

"Be careful with that one, William."

"It's the ugliest one of all," William said with a horrified sneer. Why couldn't he put it down?

"Be careful, brother. That mask is haunted."

William's breath caught in his throat. "Haunted?"

Randolph nodded. "Haunted with the evil of centuries." He pushed William's arm. "Go ahead. Try it on. I dare you. Try it on. Maybe it will persuade you to buy these wonderful faces from me."

"N-no —" William stammered. "Take it away. I can feel its evil. I can feel it right through the skin. Take it away!"

William gasped as he heard laughter. Soft, tinny laughter. Where did it come from?

He jumped back as the table started to move. No. His eyes must be playing tricks on him. The masks . . .

The table wasn't moving. The masks were wriggling and bouncing on top of one another. The sound of laughter rose till it filled the room.

The laughter was coming from the jiggling masks.

And as William gaped in shock, the masks floated up from the table. Soared up together, skin flapping, open mouths releasing peal after peal of cruel laughter.

The laughing masks formed a wall in front of William and began to bump up against him . . . bump him . . . bump him in an ugly, frightening game of tag.

"Shut up! Shut up!" The terrified man covered his ears. The harsh laughter sent chills down his back. The wall of bumping masks was too gruesome, too hideous for his eyes.

"Shut up! Stop that laughter! Get down!"

William swung his fists at them, trying to beat them down. He grabbed at the floating masks, but they pulled back out of his reach. He shot his fists forward, trying to punch them down — anything to make them stop.

But his efforts made them laugh even harder. The ugly faces leered at him, teasing him, taunting him.

William turned to his brother. Randolph stood with his arms crossed in front of him. He had an angry scowl on his face.

He grabbed William's elbow and spun him around. "I *knew* you wouldn't buy my masks!"

he screamed. "Everything I ever do is wrong! Is that what you believe? You've always been so superior — like you're so much better than me. You've always treated me like I was dirt under your fingernails."

Randolph uttered an angry cry. "You were always the talented one. The gifted mask-maker. The artist. And I was just a common thief. A beggar."

The jiggling curtain of floating masks laughed louder.

"Well, this time *I'm* the winner, William! This time, I am the one who comes out the winner. Because once and for all, I have defeated you. I have *doomed* you, brother!"

William tried to back away. But the floating masks blocked his path.

Randolph grabbed the green mask — the Haunted Mask. He gripped it in both hands. Dove forward — raised it high, and tugged the mask down over William's head.

William let out a scream. His cry was muffled inside the mask.

He could feel the mask tighten onto his face. It felt warm and dry and . . . *alive*!

"Nooooo!" He uttered another cry and grabbed at the cheeks. He struggled to pull them away from his skin. "Take this off! Randolph — help me! Take this off!"

William grappled with the mask. Why did it seem to be tightening so rapidly? Pressing itself to his skin. He struggled to see through the open eyeholes. But his vision was clouded, as if a heavy fog had invaded the room.

21

He lowered his hands to the bottom of the mask and tried to slip his fingers underneath. Tried to pry it up, away from his throat.

But no.

His hands slapped frantically at the mask, exploring, searching for the bottom, for where the mask ended and his skin began.

*It's attaching itself to me!*

The laughter of the floating masks seemed distant now. Even his own cries sounded as if they were coming from far away.

He felt a red, raging anger build in his chest.

*Is the anger coming from me? Or from the mask?*

He tore at the sides of the mask. "Randolph! Help me! Take this off!" His voice came out rough and raspy — not his voice at all.

He squinted through the eyeholes. "Randolph! You win! Take this mask off me!"

The masks giggled and bounced in front of him, a floating wall. They circled him slowly, mouths hanging open. He couldn't see his brother. Couldn't see him anywhere.

And then as he stared in growing horror, he watched the masks turn away from him. They whirled away, still laughing, and floated to the door. The open front door.

' In seconds, the masks were gone. Vanished into the night. He could still hear their laughter from outside.

"Randolph?"

He turned from the open door. He spun all around. "Randolph?"

His brother had vanished, too.

William tossed back his head and let out an animal cry. He could feel wave after wave of anger roll down his body until his chest felt about to explode.

He grabbed and slapped and tugged at the hideous mask. But he couldn't budge it. The skin of the mask had attached itself to him. It had become *his* skin now.

And the evil of the mask filled *him* with rage, a powerful fury so strong, so overwhelming, he could no longer control himself.

Bellowing his rage, William slammed the front door shut, so hard it thudded like thunder. He slapped a vase off a table, sending it crashing to the floor. Then he lifted the table in both hands and heaved it across the room into the fireplace.

He took his dining table in both hands and smashed it against his cabinet of glasses and china. He tore through the living room, slapping books off the shelves, pulling down shelves, pulling down everything that came in front of him.

He shattered the lamps with his bare hands and ripped the curtains off the walls. In minutes, his house was destroyed, piles of broken glass everywhere, broken chairs on top of shattered chinaware, paintings ripped in two.

Breathing in loud wheezes, he didn't stop — until Hansel crept into the room. The frightened dog had his ears down, his tail tucked between his legs.

"Hansel!" William roared. "Hansel!" The sight of the dog made him feel a little calmer. The dog watched him warily and wouldn't come close.

"Hansel, look what he has done to me. Randolph has doomed me. *Doomed* me!" He reached out to the dog. But Hansel whimpered and backed away.

"You don't recognize me — *do* you?" William cried. "You don't recognize me because of this evil mask."

Once again, he began tearing at the mask, pulling it, prying at it, trying to rip it away with both hands.

*Come off. Come off. Come off!*

With a terrifying burst of strength, William gave a final heave. He opened his mouth in a scream of agony as the mask tore away. It made a loud ripping sound as it ripped free.

William screamed again as unbearable pain roared over him, crippling him. And he saw the blood flow from his head.

Holding the mask, he saw the skin clinging to its inside. And he knew what he had done.

He knew.

*I've torn my FACE off with the mask!*

He dropped to his knees. The pain was too powerful. He couldn't stand.

*I've torn my face off. The only way to remove the mask.*

*And now I must wait to die.*

William gripped the mask in his fist. Chunks of his skin clung to the mask. Blood poured all around him.

*I can't let anyone else fall victim to this evil Haunted Mask.*

*I must hide it away. I must hide it so no one will ever find it.*

He staggered to his feet. His head felt as if on fire ... burning ... burning ...

He saw Hansel cowering in a corner, whimpering softly.

"You will be okay, Hansel. Someone ... a kind someone will take care of you."

It broke his heart to leave Hansel there. But William knew he had no choice. He had to protect others from the evil of this mask.

Grasping it tightly, he stumbled up the stairs to the attic. Blood flowed down his forehead. It pooled in his eyes and made it hard to see. He knew he didn't have much time.

He dropped to his knees again. His hands fumbled over an old trunk against the attic wall. The trunk was black with gold decoration and a gold latch on the front.

William flung open the lid. The smell of mothballs rose up to greet him. He peered inside. The large chest was filled with old costumes. Costumes and masks.

"Must ... hide ... the mask," he murmured, feeling himself grow weak.

He jammed the ugly mask into the trunk. Pushed it deep. Slid it under the pile of old costumes. Down ... down to the bottom. Hidden where no one would ever find it.

With a groan, William slammed the lid down. He pushed in the gold latch. Listened for the click. Used every bit of his remaining strength to shove the trunk back against the wall.

Then ...

*I must find a place to die.*

He realized he was on his knees beside the big attic closet. The deep closet that ran nearly the length of the attic.

*Yes. Perfect.*

He crawled into the closet. Allowed its darkness to swallow him up.

*I am dying. But I will guard the trunk. I will stand guard here. Guard the Haunted Mask.*

*Even after I am dead, I will keep up my watch. Death will not stop me. I will stay in this closet and do my best to keep any innocent victim from the evil of the Haunted Mask.*

The last sounds William heard were the quiet whimpers of Hansel, just outside the closet door.

# PART TWO:

# LU-ANN'S STORY

## 40 YEARS LATER

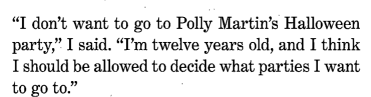

"I don't want to go to Polly Martin's Halloween party," I said. "I'm twelve years old, and I think I should be allowed to decide what parties I want to go to."

I punched the couch cushion. "Polly gives the lamest parties on Earth. No. In the universe. Her parties are so lame, they give the word *lame* a bad name."

My friend Devin O'Bannon laughed. "You're funny, Lu-Ann."

"I'm not being funny!" I screamed. "I'm serious. Why should Halloween be ruined because —"

"You've been friends with Polly since kindergarten," Devin said. He jammed a handful of popcorn into his mouth.

"You sound like my mom," I grumbled. "Just because we've known each other forever doesn't mean we're friends."

Devin said something, but his mouth was so loaded with popcorn, I couldn't understand a word he said. What a slob. But that's okay. I mean, all my friends are jokers and weirdos.

Devin and I were sitting on opposite ends of the couch in my den. We both had our feet up on the coffee table. Devin kept scooping up handfuls of popcorn from the big bowl my mom made. Half of them went into his mouth, the other half on the couch and floor.

My side of the couch was clean. I don't like popcorn. I only like sweets. I knew there was a carton of rocky road ice cream in the freezer. But I was feeling too lazy to get up and get it. Too lazy and too upset.

"You know the other thing I hate about Polly's parties?" I said.

He grinned. "Besides *everything*?"

"She makes you pay," I said. "Five dollars a person. Why do we have to pay money to be bored? I can be bored just sitting here with you."

"Thanks, Lu-Ann. You're a pal."

You can tell by the way I tease Devin that I like him a lot.

"Five dollars," I muttered.

"Well, you know Polly. She's never seen a dollar bill she didn't like."

"Guess Polly's idea of a great party game," I said with a moan.

"Spin the Bottle?"

"No. Shut up. That's too exciting. Her idea of a good game is rubbing a balloon on your forehead until the static electricity makes it stick. Then seeing who can keep the balloon on their face the longest."

Devin laughed again. "Got any balloons? We could practice."

I gave him a hard shove. "Why do you keep laughing? It isn't funny."

He spit out an unpopped kernel. Then he stuck it on my nose.

I slapped his hand away. "Why are you so immature?"

"I learned it from you."

"Could you be any less funny?"

"I could try."

I grabbed a handful of popcorn from the bowl and dropped it in his red, curly hair. He shook his head hard, sending popcorn flying all over the den.

As I said, I like Devin a lot. He's fun. Not like Polly Martin.

Polly is sweet and nice. Really. She's very smart and a total knockout with her big green eyes and dazzling smile. Like a toothpaste model or something.

Her problem is that she's soooo serious. All the time. I mean, she smiles sometimes, but I've never seen her laugh. She doesn't get jokes. She never knows when you're teasing her. She's into Green Power, and saving the bald eagles, and she's a vegetarian. You get the picture.

Not that there's anything wrong with all that. But I told you, my friends are all jokers and clowns and goof-offs. So it's hard to stay close friends with her.

"Why do you think being forced to go to Polly's Halloween party is so funny?" I asked Devin. "You have to go, too."

"No, I don't."

"Excuse me? Why don't you?"

His grin faded. He raised his eyes to the TV on the wall. We had it on with the sound off. The TV is always on in my house. Don't ask me why. There was some cooking contest on the screen, with teams of people scrambling to make cup-cakes as fast as they could.

"Lu-Ann, you might think you're the unluckiest person in the universe," Devin said. "But I am. I would *kill* to go to Polly's Halloween party."

"You're joking, right?"

"I wish." He let out a sad sigh. "My Halloween is going to be a *lot* lamer than yours."

I stared at him, waiting for him to continue.

He brushed more popcorn from his hair. "Do you know how to spell *tragic*?"

"Of course I do. I didn't have to take first grade three times like you."

"I only took it twice," he said. "My life is tragic, Lu-Ann. My Halloween will be tragic. It's the perfect word."

Devin and I talk about perfect words sometimes. He knows I want to be a writer when I'm older. I'm really good at thinking up stories. Everyone says I have an awesome imagination.

My mom says my imagination is *too* awesome. She doesn't mean that in a nice way. She wishes I was more serious, like my little brother, Mitch.

"Don't keep me in suspense, creep," I said. "Just tell me what's so tragic."

"My dad bought a pumpkin farm," he said.

"Your dad isn't a farmer. He works at an insurance company. Oh. Sorry. I mean, he *worked* at an insurance company. I know he's been looking for work. But . . . pumpkins?"

Devin rolled his brown eyes. "Tell me about it. Actually, he just leased it. It's one of those Pick-Your-Own-Pumpkin places. You know. You walk in the field and pull your own pumpkins off the vine. Big thrill, right?"

"We did that when I was five," I said. "I thought those long, twisty vines were creepy. Mitch was two and he started to cry. So we had to leave."

"I'm going to cry, too," Devin said. "But Dad thinks he's going to make a fortune selling pumpkins. It's only one week till Halloween. How many pumpkins can he sell?"

I shook my head. "Oh, wow."

"Wait," Devin said. "Here comes the tragic part. He got permission to take me out of school all week so I can help out on the farm."

"Oh, noooo," I moaned.

"Oh, yes. So where am I going to be spending Halloween? In a pumpkin patch."

"No way. No way."

"Polly's party will be a total *thrill* by comparison," Devin said, shaking his head.

His hand scraped the bottom of the popcorn bowl. "Hey, what happened to all the popcorn?"

"Very funny. Most of it's stuck to your teeth."

I was joking around, but I felt bad for him. He's not a farm kind of guy. He actually spent his first seven years in New York City. Then his dad got transferred here to Dayton, Ohio.

But Devin is a city dude.

"You're just going to rot with the pumpkins," I said sadly.

He sighed. "Thanks for trying to cheer me up."

That made us both laugh. I checked the clock on the cable box. Then I jumped to my feet. "See you when you get back," I said. "Good luck." I gave him a hard, phony handshake.

He stood up. "Lu-Ann, where are you going?" he asked as I pushed him toward the front door.

"I have to go scare my little brother now."

I tell my brother, Mitch, a scary story every
night before he goes to sleep. I just make them
up as I go along.

Mitch likes my stories and he hates them at
the same time. He doesn't really like to be
scared. He grits his teeth and shuts his fists and
pretends he's brave.

I don't want to torture the poor kid. But I
only know how to tell scary stories. That's
the only kind of story I can dream up. I guess
I just have a scary mind.

Mitch and I look alike a little bit. We both have
straight black hair and dark eyes and round

faces. I'm very thin, but he's pretty chubby. Mom says he hasn't lost his baby fat.

How do you think that line goes over with Mitch?

Not too well.

Mitch is a quiet, serious kid. He's only eight, but he likes to read endlessly long fantasy books about ancient kingdoms and dragons and battles and stuff.

He gets straight A's at Meadowdale, his elementary school. But he doesn't have a lot of friends.

I think it's because he's so quiet and shy.

We get along great even though we're so different. The only thing we fight about is breakfast — toaster waffles or toaster pancakes? He goes for waffles, and I like the pancakes. Mom says it would be silly to buy both. So . . . big fights in the supermarket.

I took Mitch into the kitchen for his nightly bedtime snack — Oreos and a glass of milk to dip them in. Then we headed upstairs. Mitch climbed into his platform bed and pulled up the covers.

Dad got him a platform bed down on the floor because he tosses and turns and rolls around a lot at night. And he was always falling out of his old bed and hurting himself.

"What's the story about?" he asked, fluffing the pillow behind his head. "Don't make it too scary, okay?"

"Okay. Not too scary," I said. Total lie.

"Tonight's story is about an evil old man. The man was so evil, he could turn himself into a snarling, clawing monster. Just by concentrating on being evil."

"What's his name?"

"His name was Mitch," I said. "Now, stop interrupting."

"No. Really. What was his name?"

"His name was Evil Boris. But people just called him Evil. Everyone was afraid of him. Every night, Evil Boris would take a walk around town and do something evil."

"Like what?"

I had the bedroom lights turned low. Mitch's dark eyes glowed in the dim light, wide with fright. His hands gripped the top of the blanket. I told the story in a whisper, just to make it scarier.

"Evil Boris liked to step on cats. Some nights he picked up big metal trash cans and poured garbage onto people's cars. He crushed birds in his bare hands. He liked to smash windows on houses just to hear the crackling glass sound. And . . . and guess what else?"

42

"What else?" Mitch asked in a tiny voice.

"Once a week, he ate someone."

"He ate people?" Mitch asked.

"He only ate kids, about your age," I said.

I almost laughed. I love making up these stories. And it makes me happy when I can think of creepy ideas like that.

"He liked to taste them first. Maybe he'd start by chewing on an arm. Sometimes he started with a leg. But the strange thing is . . . Evil Boris always saved the head for last."

Mitch made a gulping sound.

"Can you picture it?" I whispered. "Can you picture Evil Boris turning himself into a fanged monster and pulling apart someone your age . . . chewing . . . chewing . . . chewing and swallowing."

"Stop, Lu-Ann," Mitch begged. "I don't want to picture it. You said you wouldn't make it too scary."

"But I didn't tell you the scary part," I whispered. "Don't you want to hear the scary part?"

"No!" Mitch shouted. "No, I don't."

"The scary part is . . . Evil Boris lives in your closet, Mitch. He lives in the back of your clothes closet."

"Noooo!"

Uh-oh. I think I went too far. Mitch was starting to lose it.

I could see the bedcovers trembling. And I saw the dark glow of his wide, frightened eyes.

"Mitch," I said softly. I patted his shoulder. "It's just a story. It isn't true." I smoothed a hand through his thick, dark hair. "I made the whole thing up. Don't be afraid."

"Too scary," he murmured. His eyes were on the clothes closet across the bedroom.

"Go ahead. Check out the closet," I said. I tugged him up. "Go look in the closet. You'll see. It's empty. There's no one in there."

He pulled back. "I don't want to."

"It's just a story," I said. "Quick. Go look in the closet. Prove it to yourself. Then you can go to sleep."

He climbed slowly to his feet. His eyes were locked on the closet door. He crossed the room to the closet.

"Go ahead. Open it," I urged. "You'll see. No one there."

Mitch grabbed the door handle. He pulled open the door — and a hideous old man with long curled fangs and a dangling eyeball came roaring out at him.

Mitch opened his mouth in a shriek of horror.

I clapped my hands to my face. "My story!" I cried. "It *came true!*"

Mitch fell on his back, screaming.

The disgusting old man stopped. He raised both fists above his head and roared like a raging lion.

I burst out laughing.

My friend Brad Delaney pulled off the old-man mask. It took a while to tug the rubber mask off his face. He started to laugh, too. He flashed me a thumbs-up.

It didn't take Mitch long to figure out what was up. I told you he's real smart.

"You two planned this whole thing, right?"

I nodded. "Brad sneaked and hid in the closet while you were having your milk and cookies."

"Did I scare you?" Brad asked Mitch, grinning.

Mitch leaped to his feet. With an angry roar, he flung himself at me and started pounding me with both fists.

"You jerk! You jerk!"

"Okay, okay," I said, squirming away, trying to protect myself. "Stop. It was a joke, okay?"

"A stupid joke," Mitch said, breathing hard. "A stupid joke from a stupid girl."

"I guess he liked it," Brad said.

Brad has a dry sense of humor. He loves to play jokes like this on people. And he never feels bad if he scares them.

Actually, I've never seen Brad feel bad. He's always mellow. Like he's just floating on air. Know what I mean?

Brad has a lot of friends. Parents like him, too. I guess it's because he's just the happiest, easiest kid to know.

"You're not funny. You're stupid!" Mitch cried. "I hate your stories. They're too dumb. Like you."

I clamped my hands on his shoulders and pushed him away so he couldn't punch me anymore.

"Sorry," I said. "I just wanted to get you ready for Halloween. It was a joke, Mitch."

"*You're* a joke!" he screamed. "You're a stupid joke!"

"Tell you what — tomorrow night I'll tell you a *funny* story. Not a scary story. How does that sound?"

"I don't like funny stories," he growled.

I guessed he wanted to stay angry.

So I said good night, and Brad followed me out of Mitch's room and downstairs to the den. We passed Mom and Dad in the living room. They were hunched in front of the TV, playing a Wii tennis game, swinging their arms and diving for the invisible ball.

My parents love video games.

Weird, right?

Brad dropped onto an edge of the couch and picked up the empty popcorn bowl. "You didn't save me any?"

"You know Devin. He gobbled it all up. He spilled a lot on the floor. You can eat those."

"Hey, thanks."

My phone dinged. I picked it up and glanced at the screen. A text message from Polly:

WANT TO TALK ABOUT MY PARTY?

I turned the phone upside down on the coffee table. "What are we going to do about Polly's

47

party?" I asked Brad. "Should we go and just die of boredom?"

He found some popcorn between the couch cushions and popped the kernels into his mouth. "We need to liven it up," he said.

"Duh. We need to do something crazy. Something random. You know. Maybe do something to scare everyone."

He grinned. "We're good at that. Your brother will never speak to me again."

"Forget him," I said, thinking hard. "We need to do something really frightening at Polly's party and make everyone scream."

We both thought in silence for a while. Brad kept turning the rubber old-man mask between his hands. Finally, he raised his head. His eyes flashed.

"Hey, I've got an idea. What about this . . . ?"

Brad raised the ugly old-man mask. "What about this? Creepy, right?"

"Yeah," I said. "Creepy enough to make Mitch scream."

"Well ... what if we put on ugly masks like this one. Only we wear them backwards." He pulled the mask over his head and spun it around so that the face part was on the back of his head. "Then we put our clothes on backwards and we walk backwards into Polly's house and we —"

"Is that the dumbest idea you ever had?" I said. "Let's vote. I vote yes."

"Why?"

"Because if the mask is on backwards, you can't see a thing. You're totally blind."

He nodded. "Oh, yeah. You're right about that."

"Also, it's not scary at all," I said. "It just looks stupid."

Brad kept nodding. "You're right again."

"Let's think some more," I said.

Brad didn't answer. He was struggling with the mask. It was still facing backward. He tugged hard with both hands and swung it around. Then he gripped it at the top of its bald, bumpy head and pulled.

"What's your problem?" I asked.

He let out a groan. "It . . . won't . . . budge."

"Huh? Just pull harder."

He struggled and strained. I couldn't see his eyes, but I could tell he was frightened. "Brad?"

"It's stuck," he choked out. "Help me. It's . . . stuck to my skin. It's closing in on me. Lu-Ann — help! The mask . . . It's *strangling* me!"

My heart skipped a beat. Brad sounded terrified. Like a guy in a horror movie.

He jumped to his feet, tugging and grasping and pulling at the mask with both hands.

"Help! Ohh . . . help!"

With a cry, I jumped up beside him and grabbed the top of the mask. I tugged with all my strength . . .

. . . and the mask slid off Brad's face easily.

I stood there, gaping at it, holding the crumpled mask in both hands high above my head.

Brad burst out laughing. He laughed till his face turned red. "Your family sure scares easily," he said. "You're a scaredy-cat like your brother."

"Shut up," I said. I swung the mask and slapped his face with it.

That made him laugh even harder. "Maybe I'll try that joke at Polly's party."

"You didn't scare me at all," I said. Total lie.

"That was just dumb. Who would believe it?" I said. "Go home, Brad. I'll come up with something fun for the party."

He folded the mask in his hand. "We can scare Polly. I know we can," he said.

"I'll keep thinking." I walked him to the front door. I grabbed the handle and slid the door open.

And we both opened our mouths in screams of horror.

51

I gaped at the enormous, ugly gorilla in the doorway. It had to be eight feet tall! Shaggy brown
fur. Eyes glowing red, and its big belly heaving
up and down noisily.

It opened its mouth in a ferocious roar. And
I ducked away as its massive arms shot out to
grab me.

It took only two or three seconds to realize it
was someone in a gorilla costume. But those two
or three seconds were pretty frightening.

Laughing, Brad grabbed the gorilla's head —
and lifted it off its body. And there stood our
friend Marcus Wright, sweat pouring down his

face. "Hey, it's a hundred degrees in this thing. Did I scare you?"

"Not at all," I said. "In this phony costume?"

"The costume is awesome," Brad said, running his fingers through the arm fur. "Is that real fur?"

"I think it was made from a real gorilla," Marcus said.

"You're joking," I said.

He nodded. "Yes. I'm joking." He wiped sweat off his forehead with the back of a gorilla paw.

"Did you really walk all the way over here in that?" Brad asked him.

Marcus lumbered into the house. He tossed the gorilla head onto the den couch. "A few cars honked at me. But no one paid much attention."

"Who's here?" Mom called. She stepped into the den and squinted at Marcus. "Marcus, think you should see the doctor? It isn't normal for a twelve-year-old to grow that much hair."

Everyone in my family is a joker. Except Mitch, of course.

Mom and Marcus teased each other about the costume for a few minutes. I went to the kitchen and got Marcus a cold drink. He looked like he was *dying* in there.

When he isn't a gorilla, Marcus is a tall, thin African American dude with movie-star good looks (except for his ears, which are too big and flappy), a soft voice, and a high-pitched giggle that always makes me laugh.

Devin, Brad, Marcus, and I hang out together all the time, I guess because we're the only kids we know who don't take things too seriously and who like to laugh all the time, even if we're being total jerks.

Mom went back to Dad and the Wii game in the living room. Marcus plopped down in the middle of the couch. "Why don't you take off the costume?" I said.

He grinned. "Because I'm totally naked in here."

"Joking?"

He nodded. "Joking. You guys have your costumes for Polly's party? You should go to my dad's store. He has some awesome masks and costumes. Like this one."

My mouth dropped open. "Your dad opened a costume store?"

Marcus nodded. "You know. One of those pop-up stores. Over on Second Street, by the market. Just till after Halloween."

"Your dad was always into that stuff, right?" Brad asked. He picked up the gorilla mask and rubbed his hand over the snout. "Ouch! It *bit* me!"

"My dad says there used to be a famous mask store here in Dayton called William's Mask Emporium. Maybe the best mask store in the world. His dad used to take him there when he was little. And he's loved masks ever since."

Marcus picked up some popcorn from the floor and tossed it into his mouth. "My dad studies old masks. You know. From primitive people way, way back and from Africa and the Far East and from China. He's a mask freak. And now he's, like, totally pumped, selling them in his shop."

I picked a ball of fur off the couch arm. "Hey, Marcus, you're shedding."

"Does your dad have anything really scary?" Brad asked. "I mean *really* scary? Something to shake up Polly's party?"

Marcus shook his head. "Do you believe it? Another boring Halloween party, singing party songs while Polly's mother plays the accordion?"

All three of us sighed.

"I just got a great idea," Marcus said. "You and Brad go into the party first, see. You ask Polly if she heard that a big, dangerous gorilla escaped from the zoo. Then I sneak in through an upstairs window, see. And I come charging down the stairs howling and swinging my arms —"

"Lame," I interrupted.

"Awesomely lame," Brad agreed.

"My dad has these fake human arms and legs in his shop," Marcus said. "Totally real looking. What if I come running down the stairs with a human arm between my teeth?"

"Even lamer," I said. "Kids will just laugh."

Brad tossed the gorilla head to Marcus. "Let's keep thinking. There has to be a way to shake up the party."

We all agreed. There *had* to be a way.

And guess what? As it turned out, the party was a lot scarier than any of us imagined.

On Halloween night, I went to Polly's party as a vampire. I knew there would be a lot of other vampires, but I didn't care.

I painted my face white, put black circles around my eyes, smeared on black lipstick, and painted a trickle of bright red blood down one side of my mouth onto my chin. I wore a black long-sleeved top and a long, flowing black skirt of my mom's.

Polly's house is two blocks from mine, so I walked. It was a cold October night. Clouds covered the moon. Trees whispered and shivered in a gusting wind that swirled my skirt around me as I made my way along the sidewalk.

I saw groups of kids trick-or-treating. They were running excitedly up to houses, laughing and collecting candy and showing off their costumes. They were having fun.

I sighed. I knew my night wouldn't be as fun as theirs.

Polly had two fat, glowing jack-o'-lanterns on her front stoop. One had a fiery yellow grin on its carved face, the other a menacing frown. All the lights in the house were on. I could hear music pouring out, but I didn't recognize it.

I stepped into the living room. It was already jammed with kids in costumes. I quickly spotted two more vampires. They both had fangs. I'd totally forgotten about fangs.

How *could* I?

I saw green-faced monsters and a Frankenstein with bolts in his head. I pushed my way past weird purple and blue creatures. One of them had two heads. Three boys wore animal heads. Were they cows? I couldn't tell.

The living room was so full it was hard to walk anywhere. I kept bumping into people as I searched for Polly. Polly was always a princess in a white bride's dress and the same sparkly silver tiara every year.

But I couldn't find her.

I searched for Marcus in his gorilla costume and Brad in his ugly old-man gear. No sign of them.

"Hey — sorry." A curly-horned beast bumped into me hard, nearly knocking me over.

How come I didn't recognize anyone?

The music was strange. Not really party music. Kind of slow and sad with lots of violins.

*That's not the kind of music Polly usually plays. She plays bouncy, babyish music.*

"Have you seen Polly?" I asked a ghost in a long bedsheet.

The ghost stared back at me through two ragged eyeholes.

"Where is Polly's mom?" I asked.

The ghost just stared and didn't reply.

"Hey, everyone, we're going to play *Eat the Wheel*," a voice from the front of the room shouted. I couldn't see her, but I knew it wasn't Polly's voice.

"*Eat the Wheel*," someone repeated. "Cool. *Eat the Wheel. Eat the Wheel.*"

What kind of stupid game was that? How come I'd never heard of it?

*Polly? Where are you?*

*And where are my friends?*

An eight-foot-tall gorilla shouldn't be too hard to spot in a crowd.

Polly's mom always stood at the front door to greet everyone and collect the five dollars. I turned back to the door. Some kids in yellow-green insect costumes were entering. But no sign of Mrs. Martin.

And no sign of her accordion, which she always leaned at the side of the fireplace.

Where was she?

"*Eat the Wheel*?" a boy beside me said. "Where do we get our tri-wiggles? Who has the tri-wiggles?"

I suddenly felt dizzy. I didn't understand what he was saying. And I'd never heard of that game. Had Polly found some kind of new game for everyone to play? That wasn't at all like her.

"Have you seen Polly?" I asked another girl vampire.

She opened her mouth and made her fangs poke out.

"Polly?" I repeated. "I can't find Polly."

The other vampire said something in a voice too soft to hear.

Two boys in pirate costumes started to argue. As they raised their voices, I realized I didn't understand their language. I take Spanish in school, but it wasn't Spanish. It was a weird language with a lot of clicking and whistling.

A group of kids suddenly started to sing. They were also singing in a language I'd never heard.

Kids laughed as if it was the funniest song ever.

I shut my eyes. I tried to cover my ears with my hands. I suddenly didn't feel well at all.

This was totally upsetting. No Polly. No friends. No one I recognized. All talking about some weird game and talking and singing in a strange, funny-sounding language.

*Am I at the wrong party?*

I knew that was impossible. I knew Polly's house almost as well as my own.

So what was happening?

The room suddenly grew silent. The singing and talking stopped. The music stopped.

I opened my eyes in time to see the kids move into a circle. Without saying a word, they formed a wide circle around me.

They were all staring at me through their masks, glaring menacingly. I didn't have a chance to move. They tightened the circle around me.

And started to circle me, moving slowly at first, then faster. The circle of weird, cos- tumed kids — all strangers — whirled around me. And as I gaped, frozen in horror, they began to chant:

*"Pippa pippa wah wah wah*
*Pippa wah pippa wah*
*Pippa pippa wah wah."*

What did it mean? Why were they chanting at me? Staring at me so angrily?

I spun around, searching for an escape. But the circle of chanting, moving kids was too tight. I couldn't get away.

*"Pippa pippa wah wah wah*
*Pippa wah pippa wah*
*Pippa pippa wah wah."*

"No — please!" I shouted in a high, trembling voice. "Please — what do you *want*? Why are you *doing* this?"

The circle slowed down. The chanting stopped. I stared in horror, my hands over my ears.

And then I uttered a hoarse cry as they all grabbed the sides of their heads.

They grabbed their heads — *and lifted them off their bodies!*

"Oh, nooo," I moaned. "Nooooo."

They pulled their heads off their shoulders. Held them high.

I stared at the empty shoulders. At the roomful of headless kids.

Stared in shock at the costumed kids, all holding their heads high above their bodies.

And then suddenly, the heads all began to scream.

"No! Stop! Stop!" I pleaded. But I couldn't hear myself over their shrill, terrifying siren screams.

I felt a tug at my arm. "Huh?"

I flinched in fright. Who was grabbing at me?

I gazed down — and saw my brother, Mitch. He was pulling my arm and crying. Tears ran down his red face.

"Help me, Lu-Ann," he cried. "Help me."

He had to shout over the screaming heads.

"Help me! Please, Lu-Ann — help me!"

"Help me, Lu-Ann," Mitch said in a tiny voice. "Help me. I can't get the toothpaste open."

*Huh?*

I blinked. My eyelids were heavy and dry. From sleep?

Mitch poked the toothpaste tube in my face. I gazed around. My bedroom. Gray light washing in from the window. My clothes from yesterday tossed in the middle of the floor.

"Sorry, Mitch." I took the tube from him and twisted the top off. "I had a nightmare. A very scary nightmare."

He grinned. "Was it about a creepy old man who lives in the closet?"

"No. It was different. About a weird Halloween party."

"Ha-ha. You *deserve* nightmares. You give *me* nightmares all the time." He squeezed a dab of toothpaste on his finger and rubbed it on my nose.

I grabbed for him, but he dodged away and tore out of the room.

I sat up slowly, rubbing off the toothpaste. I thought about the nightmare.

"Well, I asked for it," I murmured. "I asked for a scary party at Polly's place. But that was *too* scary."

Luckily, dreams don't come true.

Party time. Polly's mom greeted me at the front door.

She wore the tall, pointy black witch's hat she wears every year. Her long fingernails had black polish, and her mouth was lipsticked black.

"Hi, Lu-Ann, aren't you adorable!" she gushed. "Let me take a look at you, sweetie-pie." She took my arms and spread them out so she could study my costume. "Let me guess. Are you a witchypoo, too?"

She talks to everyone like they're all five years old.

"No, I'm a vampire."

She raised a hand to the side of her face. "So many vampires this year. You don't drink *real blood*, do you?"

She laughed. That was a great joke for her.

"Only for dessert," I said. Then I laughed, just in case she believed me.

She's actually a very nice person, and she's a good mom. She lets Polly have sleepovers at her house all the time. And Polly can stay up as late as she wants, even on school nights. And Mrs. Martin is always having parties for everyone in Polly's class.

If only the parties weren't so dull and babyish.

I handed her the five-dollar admission fee. Then I stepped into the crowded living room and waved to Polly, who was dressed in her princess outfit.

I saw Marcus, the huge gorilla, beating his chest and bellowing by the food table. The kids around him seemed to be enjoying his act.

I spotted the dreaded accordion tilted against the wall near the fireplace. Several kids were hunched on chairs against the far wall. I knew they were complaining about how dull the party was, even though it had just started.

Polly had black-and-orange streamers strung over the living-room ceiling. And several tiny, grinning, glowing jack-o'-lanterns in a row across the mantel. A big black-and-orange sign had been hung in one of the front windows. It read:

HAVE A HAPPY HOWL-O-WEEN!

On the food table, I saw a tray of pumpkin-shaped cookies and a big punch bowl filled with some kind of orange liquid. Brad stood with a cup in his hand. I think he was trying to figure out how to drink through his rubber old-man mask.

"Does anyone want to play *Twister*?" Polly shouted.

"Oh, yes," her mother chimed in. "Wouldn't *Twister* be fun in Halloween costumes? That would be so funny. Any volunteers?"

A few kids groaned. I think we all remembered trying to play *Twister* in our costumes last year. It was a disaster. A lot of costumes got ripped and pulled off. And there were at least two fights.

"I have a better idea," Polly shouted.

"Listen to Polly, people!" her mother cried. "Polly has a fun idea."

"See all those orange and black balloons in the corner?" Polly said, pointing. "Let's everyone take a balloon. Here. I'll show you what to do."

She picked up an orange balloon and started to rub it on her forehead. "See? You rub the balloon several times till it sticks to your mask. We'll all do it at the count of three, and we'll see who can keep their balloon on the longest."

"And we'll have a wonderful prize for the winner!" her mother added. "A big bag of candy corn."

"I don't believe it," I groaned. "She's actually making everyone play this dumb game."

I grabbed Brad and pulled him across the room to Marcus. "I can't take this," I said. "I just can't."

"Lu-Ann, don't you want to win the candy corn?" Marcus joked.

"Shut up." I gave him a push. "Come on, guys. Let's get out of here."

"Out of here? Where?" Brad asked.

"Away," I said. I pushed them both. "Come on. Follow me. Let's go upstairs. Maybe it's more interesting up there."

I didn't care where we were going. I just knew we had to get away from the balloon game and the babyish party.

The two boys followed me up the stairs. At the end of the hall, I saw another set of stairs. "Let's go." We ran down the hall and climbed the steep, wooden steps.

"The attic," I murmured. I fumbled on the wall till I found a light switch. I clicked it, and a yellow ceiling light flickered on.

I blinked, waiting for my eyes to adjust to the dim light.

It was a long, low room, filled with cartons and old furniture and stacks of newspapers and magazines. I saw a closet against one wall. The single window at the end of the room rattled from the wind outside.

"Creepy," Marcus said, pulling off his gorilla mask.

"It's just an attic," I said.

"Hot up here," Brad complained. "Hot and kind of damp." He tugged off his old-man mask and wiped sweat off his face.

"At least there aren't any balloons," I said. My voice sounded tiny in the long, stuffy room. I had to squint. The ceiling light didn't send down much light.

I walked over to a bunch of old paintings leaning against the wall. The floorboards creaked with every footstep. The paintings were covered in dust. I could barely see what was painted on them. Scenes from other countries, I guessed.

Brad searched through a stack of old *Life* magazines. "Yuck. These magazines stink. And look. They've got little yellow worms crawling all over them. Sick."

"Ouch." Marcus bumped his ankle trying to walk past an old bed frame. "It's more boring up here than the party," he said. "Maybe we should go back . . . ?"

"Wait," I said. "Check this out."

I gazed down at an old chest, black with gold decorations. It looked like a pirate chest. I bumped it with my leg, and the big clasp on the front snapped open.

"Maybe it's filled with rubies and sapphires and diamonds," I said. "Pirate booty."

The boys stepped up beside me. The three of us hoisted up the heavy, spotted lid.

"Ugh." A sour, musty smell floated up from the chest. We all stared down into it. No jewels.

"Just moth-eaten old clothes?" Brad said. He took a step back.

"No. Check it out," I said. I pulled out a red pair of pants and spread it out. It looked like red overalls, only it had a pointed tail hanging down from the back.

Marcus bent down and pulled out a red object that had been tucked beneath it. He held it up. "A mask. Wow, it's super ugly. It looks totally evil. Some kind of devil, I think." He held it up over the red overalls.

"It's an old Halloween costume," Brad said. "Weird. Look. The chest is filled with old Halloween costumes." He bent down and pulled out a long, furry black suit. He tossed it to the floor and pulled up an armload of other costumes.

"Hey, let me see that one," Marcus said. He

held it up. "Is this real leopard skin? And, oh, wow, I don't believe this mask." The rubber mask looked kind of like a hippo, only it had three eyes.

"Yuck. This stuff *smells*!" I said, holding my nose.

"I don't care. It's cool," Brad said. "We can scare everyone downstairs with these costumes." He tugged off his costume and pulled the long black furry suit on.

Marcus grabbed the red devil costume and started to put it on.

"There's something at the bottom of the trunk," I said. "Buried under all the costumes." I leaned over the side and pulled out the ugliest mask I'd ever seen.

It was a sick green color. It looked kind of like an insect head with a smooth skull and pointy ears and big eyeholes. The mouth was lined with two rows of jagged, sharp teeth.

I held it in front of my face. "What do you think?"

"I don't see the difference," Marcus joked.

"Actually, it's an improvement," Brad added.

"Shut up," I said. I picked up an ugly green costume to go with the mask. It had bumps all over it, like a reptile. "Totally cool." I started to pull it on.

Brad found a creepy mask, too. It looked like a bald man with his mouth frozen open in a scream. The top of the head was split open, and bright red blood appeared to flow down both sides of his face.

"I like this dude," he said. "Looks a lot like my dad when he cuts himself shaving."

"Looks a lot more like your mom!" Marcus said.

All three of us burst out laughing.

"We're going to look totally awesome," I said. "When we go back downstairs —"

I stopped because I heard a sound. Was it a cough?

We all froze. And listened.

Yes. I heard hoarse breathing.

And then the soft thud of footsteps.

"Who's there?" I called. "Is someone up here?"

No answer.

The hoarse breathing grew louder.

"Who's up here?" I called.

Then the light went out.

"Who — who's there?" My voice cracked.

My heart started to pound like a drum machine. My skin suddenly tingled all over.

Brad and Marcus didn't move.

The floorboards squeaked under the soft pad of footsteps. The hoarse breathing was so nearby. Rapid, excited breathing.

"You — you're not scaring us!" I choked out. A total lie.

I took a few steps forward. Maybe I could make it to the stairs before our silent visitor attacked.

I let out a cry as I stumbled over something on the floor. Something soft. Something alive. "Nooooooo!"

I fell and hit my knee hard on the wooden floorboards. Pain shot through my body.

"Th-there's a creature up here," I managed to whisper.

"I can't see it. It's so dark," Marcus whispered back. "What happened to the light?"

The creature was breathing noisily now. Whatever it was, it knew it had us trapped.

I forced myself to my feet. My knee throbbed.

I stumbled forward. Bumped into something hard. And a white light flashed on.

A floor lamp. I'd bumped into a floor lamp. And turned it on.

I spun around, ready to face the creature. And burst out laughing.

It was Buzzy. Polly's big, friendly black Lab.

Marcus and Brad let out long sighs of relief. Then they dropped down beside me on the floor. And the three of us petted Buzzy and told him what a good dog he was.

I glanced up at the ceiling light. The old bulb must have gone out. The light switch was too high for Buzzy to bump.

Buzzy panted and drooled and seemed to enjoy

all the attention. But then the dog froze. His ears stood straight up. He arched his back. I could actually see the fur on his back stand up.

Buzzy jumped to his feet. His brown eyes stared at something across the room. His entire body went stiff.

"Look at him," Marcus whispered. "He's like that hunting dog my family used to have. It's like he's spotted his prey."

"Prey? What kind of prey is in this attic?" I said. I felt my skin tingle with fear again.

The big dog was staring at the closet against the wall. He took a few timid steps toward it. His ears went down. He lowered his head — and started to whimper.

"What's wrong, Buzzy?" I asked. "What's frightening you?" I tried to pet his back, but he shook me off. I saw his body tremble. He kept his head down, staring at the closet, and whimpered like a child.

"There's something in the closet," Brad said. "Something scaring him."

"Well, what could it be?" I said. I took a deep breath, worked up my courage. Then I crossed the attic to the closet, gripped the door handle, and pulled it open.

The attic rang with our screams as a hideous old man came roaring out of the closet. He was half skeleton, half human. Most of the skin was missing on his face, and I could see the yellowed bone of his skull.

His eyes were sunk deep in their sockets. His nose was missing. Just a hole on the front of his face. His mouth was an open, empty gash.

He wore a ratty black cape and baggy, torn black trousers. He was barefoot. One foot had skin. The other was just bones.

He came screaming out at us, bony hands reaching in front of him.

No time to escape. He grabbed me by the shoulders and tightened his grip until I gasped.

"*The mask . . .*" His voice was a hoarse crackle from somewhere deep in his throat. "*It's haunted. . . .*"

"Let me go!" I shrieked. I pulled back — and slipped easily from his bony fingers. I stumbled backward into Brad and Marcus.

"*Haunted . . . The mask . . .*" the hideous man groaned. His sunken eyes studied each of us. His cracked lips kept moving, working over his toothless gums.

"Leave us alone!" I screamed. "Go away — *please!*" I could still feel the iron-hard grip of his bony fingers on my shoulders.

He nodded solemnly. I could see cracks in the top of his head. "*Listen to an old ghost. . . . Listen to a lonely old ghost. . . . The mask . . .*"

"Noooo!" I screamed. I grabbed the handle and *slammed* the closet door shut.

The three of us pressed our shoulders to the door, hoping to keep him inside. Heart pounding, I expected the door to come flying open and the old ghost to come raging out at us.

But no. The door didn't budge. The only sound was our rapid, wheezing breaths.

We darted away from the closet. "He's . . .

gone." I hugged myself to stop my shivers. "It's . . . just like my story," I murmured.

Both boys turned to me. "What story?" Marcus asked.

"An evil old ghost living in a closet. It's like a story I made up for Mitch the other night. But how can that *be*?"

I didn't want to think about it. It was just too weird. "Let's get out of here." I ran to the stairs. My legs were shaking. "We have to tell Polly. We — we have to warn everyone. We have to tell them there's a ghost in the attic."

I grabbed the ugly green mask and pulled it on. Weird. It felt strangely warm. Not rubbery. Soft and warm as human skin.

"Let's go," Marcus said from behind the red devil mask. He helped Brad pull on the bald-man mask with its head split open and bleeding. "If these old costumes don't scare everyone, we'll *totally* terrify them when we tell them about the ghost in the attic."

My mask felt a little tight and uncomfortable. I tugged at it, trying to stretch it a bit as I raced down the stairs to the party. Brad and Marcus followed close behind me.

Halfway down, I saw that the balloon game had ended. Polly and her mother were handing out plastic squirt guns. I saw a row of candles on the table. I knew this was the old squirt-out-the-candles game we've played since we were five.

Big whoop.

I stopped almost at the bottom of the stairs.

"There's a . . ." I started to tell them about the ghost upstairs. But I stopped. I don't know why.

Instead, I lifted the green, scaly arms of my costume. And I roared: *"You're all DOOMED!"*

Behind me, Marcus and Brad let out hideous screams, shrieks like from a bad horror movie.

*"DOOMED!"* I cried at the top of my lungs. My voice sounded strange, kind of raspy through the ugly green mask. *"You're DOOMED!"*

Polly dropped the bundle of squirt guns in her hands. The kids all turned to the stairway. I heard a few kids scream.

"Who are you?" Polly's mom shouted. Her eyes were wide with alarm. "How did you get upstairs? Do you belong at this party?"

"We've haunted the attic for one hundred years!" Marcus boomed in a creepy old man's voice.

"Now we will haunt YOU!" Brad yelled.

"I will call the police if you are crashing this party," Polly's mom said, frowning at us. "If you do not leave —"

"That's Brad," a boy said, pointing. "I recognize his voice."

"Yes. Brad and Marcus," another boy chimed in.

Polly's mom looked very relieved. She laughed. "And is that Lu-Ann in the green mask with all those horrible teeth? You three fooled us. You gave us a good scare."

Kids all started talking at once. They stared at the old masks and costumes we were wearing.

"Take off your masks so we can see it's really you," Polly said.

Brad reached for his mask with both hands. He started to pull it off, gripping the split halves of the head. "Hey —" he uttered a startled cry.

The room grew quiet.

Brad tugged again. "I . . . can't . . . get it off," he groaned.

On the step above him, Marcus was pulling hard on the red devil mask. "Whoa. Mine won't come off, either."

I turned and watched both boys struggle and strain and tug.

"It's stuck to my skin!" Brad cried. "Help me! It's totally stuck to me!"

"Please — help!" Marcus wailed. "I'm trapped in this thing. It won't let go! It won't let go of me!"

My breath caught in my throat. *This can't be happening.*

I spun around, grabbed the sides of Brad's mask, and pulled up hard.

A few kids were shouting and screaming. Most of them just stood frozen in shocked silence.

Finally, Brad and Marcus both started to laugh.

"Gotcha!" Marcus shouted. "Did you really believe us?"

Brad slid off his mask. He tossed it into the

crowd of kids. "You guys are too easy to fool!" he declared.

Brad and Marcus bumped knuckles and slapped each other high-fives.

"Just a joke," Polly's mom announced, as if everyone didn't already get it. "What a hilarious Halloween joke. You certainly got everyone's attention."

Marcus and Brad were smiling at me. "Success!" Marcus exclaimed. "We shook up this party."

"We have to tell you all about the *real* ghost," Brad said.

"Yeah, sure," someone groaned. "Like we're going to believe you now."

The voices faded into the background. I suddenly felt a little scared.

I could feel my mask moving. Kind of changing.

A heavy feeling of dread formed in the pit of my stomach. I didn't want to believe it, but the mask was growing warmer and warmer. And I could feel it shrinking, tightening to my face.

Brad and Marcus had pulled a joke about how their masks wouldn't come off. But this was no joke. This was really happening to me.

I reached my hands up to my neck and searched for the bottom of the mask. I knew I couldn't tug it off from the top. I had to grab the bottom and slide it up. Pull the mask off from the bottom.

But, wait. No. Oh, please, no.

My hands fumbled at my neck. I slid them up, then down, then back up.

Where was the bottom of the mask?

I couldn't find the place where the mask ended and my skin began.

*The mask has melted itself to my skin.*

My hands were shaking like crazy now. My panic was making my whole body shake.

I felt the mask tighten some more. It was *alive.* Yes. The old mask was *alive.*

I felt it moving, warming up, stretching itself, melting to my skin.

"HELP ME!" The scream burst from my throat.

I pulled and strained frantically at the mask. But it was no longer a mask. It was *attached* to me. It was *part* of me.

"Help me! I really need help! The mask — it's melted to my face!"

Brad and Marcus burst out laughing.

Other kids started to laugh. Everyone stared at me, smiling, laughing, joking.

"No — really!" I wailed. "I really need help! This old mask — it . . . it's ALIVE!"

More laughter.

"Oh, please, Lu-Ann," Polly's mom said, chuckling and shaking her head. "The boys already pulled that joke. Take off the mask and come join everyone."

"I can't!" I screamed. My voice sounded tinny, hoarse inside the mask. It wasn't my voice at all. Somehow, even my voice had become ugly, monstrous.

"I can't take it off!" I wailed again. "Please — I'm not joking! Somebody help me!"

I gripped it with both hands and pulled with all my might.

Kids laughed. Marcus and Brad were laughing, too.

And suddenly, my fear gave way to something else. Suddenly, I was no longer terrified.

Now I was *angry*. Now a burning, furious anger swept over me.

I felt about to blow up. Yes. Explode. Explode in screaming anger.

*What am I going to do? I've never felt anything like this in my life!*

I balled my hands into tight fists. I clenched my jaw. I felt every muscle in my body tense — so hard I could barely breathe.

As my anger boiled, I made one last attempt

to pull off the mask. I tore at it. Scraped it with my nails. Ripped my fingers at the eyeholes.

But there were no eyeholes. There was no mask. It was my face now. The hideous, sharp-toothed, green scaly face was *my face.*

# 12

I couldn't hold myself in any longer. I felt it erupt inside me. My body churned — as if I were *vomiting* my anger!

An animal roar burst from deep down. A terrifying, menacing bellow of horror. So loud and furious, it even frightened *me*.

But I couldn't stop the anger. I lost myself. Lost Lu-Ann. Lost myself in the boiling sea of anger. Sank into it. Sank deep into the red, blinding red of my hate and fury.

I raised my eyes to the costumed kids in Polly's living room. They were still laughing. The idiots.

The stupid jerks. They thought I was putting on some kind of show.

*I'll show them it isn't pretend.*

I attacked. I leaped over the banister and landed on a boy in a mummy costume. We both toppled to the floor. I wrapped my hands around his throat and squeezed until he squeaked.

Then I jumped to my feet. I lowered my shoulder and ran into a couple of girls. They fell backward and slammed into a wall.

I tossed back my head and let out another furious roar.

Kids weren't laughing anymore. Now they were screaming. Now they were backing away in fright.

Ha.

I leaped up and ripped streamers off the ceiling. I knocked over a table and sent a lamp crashing to the floor.

"Stop! Stop! Lu-Ann — stop!" I heard Mrs. Martin screaming.

I grabbed a pumpkin pie off the food table and smashed it in her face. Then I hoisted up the food table in both hands and tipped it on its side.

All the food and drinks slid to the floor. The punch bowl shattered into a million pieces, sending the orange drink pooling over the carpet.

Kids screamed in terror. I saw a couple of girls run out the front door.

Polly had a phone to her ear. Was she calling the police?

I didn't care. I couldn't control myself. Couldn't control my red rage.

I ripped a painting off the wall and smashed its glass frame against the banister.

Kids shrieked and screamed.

I loved it!

Polly's mom was still wiping pie off her face. I heaved a vase at the wall. She spun toward me and sprang forward, trying to tackle me.

With a cry, I dodged past her outstretched arms. I took a flying leap and dove right through the living-room window.

Glass shattered and crashed all around me.

I landed on my knees. Then I climbed quickly to my feet. And took off, roaring down the street, screaming like a crazed animal.

The cool night air felt good on my hot face. I was panting hard, my chest heaving up and down.

I ran to the street. Stopped at the bottom of Polly's driveway. And ripped the mailbox off its pole. I threw it at the house.

My shoes slapped the pavement as I ran along the sidewalk. I knew I should stop running. I knew I should try to fight this anger.

But it was too powerful. I wasn't strong enough to battle it.

I felt sooooo ANGRY.

I saw three little kids trick-or-treating at a brightly decorated house across the street. I waited till they were halfway down the front lawn. Then I ran up to them, roaring.

I grabbed their candy bags and ripped them to pieces. Candy went flying over the grass. Two of the kids started to cry.

That made me laugh.

I tipped over a bike in the next driveway. I bent down, grabbed a sprinkler hose — and ripped the hose in two with my bare hands. Water went gushing over the lawn.

*What next? What next?*

I turned the corner and ran, searching for more trick-or-treaters to scare.

I slowed down when I heard sounds behind me. Heavy footsteps on the pavement. I heard a shout.

Who was coming after me?

I spun around — and saw Marcus and Brad running fast.

"Lu-Ann — wait up! Lu-Ann!" Marcus called breathlessly.

"Stop! We want to help you!" Brad cried.

*"Help me?"* I grunted in a raspy voice that wasn't mine. *"You want to help me? Here's what I think about your help!"*

I grabbed Brad and sank my teeth into his shoulder.

He screamed, more in surprise than in pain.

91

I laughed and let him go. I could feel thick drool running down my chin. I slid my fangs together, grinding them, preparing to bite again.

"Lu-Ann — just stop," Marcus said, motioning me back with both hands. "You need help."

*"You'll need help when I'm finished with you,"* I snarled. I raised both hands and curled them like claws, ready to scratch their eyes out.

*What am I doing?*

*These are my FRIENDS.*

"Lu-Ann — let us help you," Marcus said.

Brad rubbed his shoulder where I had bitten him. "We'll take you home," he said. "Your parents can call a doctor."

I tossed back my head and roared in reply.

The sound frightened them. They both took a step back.

"Is it the mask?" Brad asked. "Is the mask making you do these things?"

"We'll help you take it off," Marcus said. His voice trembled.

*"It can't come off,"* I growled. *"It's my face now."* I took a step toward them, curled hands still raised. *"What's the matter? It's not pretty enough for you?"*

They glanced at each other and didn't reply. I could see they were terrified.

*Should I bite them again?*

No. This was getting boring. I needed more excitement. After all, it was Halloween night. And I had more anger to burn, more damage to do.

"Lu-Ann, please —" Marcus held his hand out to me. "Let us take you home."

I slapped his hand away, spun around, and took off. I ran through three front yards, then an empty lot.

I turned back. Were they following me? No. They had given up.

*Great friends. I should have bitten them both.*

I turned a corner and kept running. My chest was burning, but I felt as if I could run forever.

Run and roar forever.

The houses ended, and I saw a row of small shops across the street. They were all dark except for the store at the end.

As I crossed the street, I read the neon sign over the door. MASKS & MORE.

The front window was brightly lit with rows of ugly masks on display. A sign read: MEXICAN DAY OF THE DEAD MASKS.

Marcus's dad's store. Mr. Wright. This had to be his Halloween store.

I stopped and stared into the window.

*Mr. Wright has studied old masks. He is an expert on old masks.*

93

*Maybe he can help me. Maybe he can help me get this mask off.*

*He HAS to help me!*

I grabbed the door handle so hard, I ripped it off the door. With a low growl, I tossed it aside. Then I went roaring into the store.

It was a tiny shop with costumes hanging from metal racks, jammed on both sides of the narrow aisle. A jungle of costumes stretching into the aisle.

Masks were hung side by side on three walls, nearly from floor to ceiling. Dozens and dozens of animal masks and monster masks and funny masks and scary masks. A glass display case held all kinds of shiny badges, belts, tiaras, and wands.

There was barely room to walk. The lights were dim, casting strange shadows over the rows of empty-eyed masks. I squinted to the back of the store. No sign of Mr. Wright.

I let out a rasping roar. *"Anybody here?"*

Costumes scraped against one another as if they were alive. Masks grinned down at me.

*"Anybody here? Mr. Wright?"*

He appeared from behind a pile of red and black costumes in the back. He was carrying a skeleton mask in one hand and a can of Coke in the other.

Startled, he dropped the soda can when he saw me. It clanged to the floor and Coke spilled over his shoes.

Mr. Wright is a big man, tall and wide and nearly bald. He wears thick, black-rimmed glasses that are always falling down his nose. He was dressed in dark denim jeans and a white turtleneck sweater under an open brown sports jacket.

He bent to pick up the Coke can. Then he stood and stared at me. "Hello?"

*"Mr. Wright, it's me, Lu-Ann,"* I growled. *"Help me. I need your help!"*

He squinted through his glasses at the mask over my face. "Who are you? What did you say?"

I glimpsed myself in the mirror beside him. My face was green, the skin cracked and lined like lizard skin. My eyes were huge and bloodred.

My two rows of fangs poked from my open mouth with drool running down my chin.

*"Help me — please. Can you help me?"*

He didn't say a word. He stood there staring hard at me. Studying my face. Studying the mask.

After a long while, he raised his big hand and pointed at me. "Get out!" he boomed. "Get out of here! Out of my store — now! You're evil! *Evil!*"

"No, Mr. Wright," I begged in my ugly, rasping voice. "It's me — Lu-Ann."

"Out!" he screamed. He took a step toward me, still waving his finger in the air. "Out! Out of my store!"

"BUT I NEED HELP!" I roared.

My rage took over. I started grabbing masks off the wall and ripping them in half with my bare hands. I knocked over two racks of costumes. I smashed my fist through the glass display case.

Mr. Wright came charging at me. He had his big arms spread wide to grab me. "Out! Out of here!"

I had no choice. I leaped over the costumes I had spilled into the aisle. And I took off running. Back onto the street.

Mr. Wright filled the doorway to the shop. He

shook his fist at me. "Go away! Go away! I don't want your evil near me."

"It's me!" I screamed. "Lu-Ann! Please — listen to me. Your son Marcus is my good friend. You know me. I am Lu-Ann. Really. Can't you help me get this mask off?"

I couldn't see his face. He was a big shadow with the store light shining behind him. "Maybe you *used* to be Lu-Ann," he shouted. "But now you are the Haunted Mask. And I know all about the evil you bring."

"No. It's still me!" I insisted. "I'm still Lu-Ann. Please, help me. How ... how do I take this mask off?"

"Do you really want me to tell you how to remove the Haunted Mask — or is this some kind of trick?"

"No. It's not a trick," I said. "Please tell me." A gob of drool ran down my chin and spattered the pavement at my feet. "What do you know about this mask? How do I take it off?" I grunted. "Tell me how to take it off." I tugged at the sides of my face, tugged the soft, warm, scaly green skin.

He stood there for a long moment, arms crossed, blocking the doorway.

"The Haunted Mask cannot be taken off," he said.

*Can't be taken off?*

I stared at him for a moment. Then I raised both fists above my head and let out a furious wail.

He backed into his shop. "I've read a lot about the Haunted Mask. It was given to a shop owner named William. The day he got it, he and the mask disappeared and were never seen again. According to legend, the mask cannot be taken off — unless . . ."

"Unless?" I croaked.

"Only an act of unbelievable kindness can remove it," he said. "That's all I know. Now go away. Go and take your evil with you." He slammed the door to the shop.

"Kindness? You want kindness?" I cried. "I'll show you kindness."

I picked up a big stone from the street and heaved it at his shop door. It made a loud *thunk*, then bounced off.

Then I ran down the row of darkened shops, breaking windows, laughing like a crazed hyena . . . laughing . . . laughing and shattering glass . . . running full speed down the empty street.

I was a prisoner of the Haunted Mask, a prisoner of its evil.

But under all the anger and rage, I was still Lu-Ann. Still frightened, terrified Lu-Ann.

*What's going to happen to me?* I wondered. *How evil am I going to get?*

I couldn't stop. I smashed the window of the last store on the block and kept running. A burglar alarm clanged in one of the stores. And somewhere in the distance, I heard a siren approaching.

I darted across the street and ran into the darkness of a small, heavily wooded park. Running beneath the trees, I struggled to think. Struggled to think like Lu-Ann.

*An act of kindness.*

*I have to fight the power of the mask and do an act of kindness.*

*The only way to free myself . . .*

The mask fought back. It tried to drown out these thoughts with thoughts of evil, of hurting people, of smashing and wrecking everything in my path.

Those angry feelings were overpowering. I couldn't control them. And when I saw the little girl sitting on the curb, I felt the anger bubble up in me, and I knew she was in big trouble.

From me.

She was dressed in a princess costume. But her sparkly tiara lay on the ground next to her. She had her head in her hands. Under the streetlight, I saw her dark hair bobbing up and down, and I knew she was crying.

I opened my mouth to roar, to terrify her.

But somehow I choked it back. And I dropped down beside her on the curb.

It took her a while to notice me. Finally, she raised her head, sniffling, and wiped tears off her cheeks.

"What's wrong?" I whispered.

"Lost," she replied in a trembling voice.

"You're lost?"

She nodded, still wiping away tears. She had her eyes down. She hadn't seen my hideous face yet.

"I was with all these kids. But I can't find them now. I don't know where they went."

"And you don't know how to get home?"

"No. I'm lost." Her shoulders quivered. More tears poured from her big, dark eyes.

"Don't worry. I'll help you," I said softly in my hoarse, raspy voice. "I'll take you home. No problem."

Her eyes went wide. "You will?"

"Yes."

*An act of kindness.*

*An act of kindness to get rid of this evil mask.*

"Thank you," she said in a tiny voice. And then she turned to me.

She looked at me for the first time.

Her smile vanished, and her mouth trembled, then opened wide in a scream of horror.

"You're so UGLY!" she shrieked. She jumped to her feet. She tried to run. But she wasn't fast enough.

I grabbed her by her tiny shoulders. *"Where are you going, little girl?"* I snarled. *"I'm going to help you. I'm going to help you eat all your candy!"*

I snatched her trick-or-treat bag from her hands. Shoved her aside.

Then I frantically ripped the bag to pieces.

Candy bars flew everywhere. I grabbed them as they fell. Swiped them off the ground — and jammed them into my mouth, grinding them up . . . gobbling   them . . . gobbling — wrappers and all — crushing them in my huge, pointed teeth.

The little girl was sobbing loudly now. Her face was all wet and twisted in fear.

It made me laugh. I spotted her sparkly tiara on the ground. Picked it up and plunked it on my smooth, bald head.

Then I ran off, tore full speed down the street. Laughing my head off. Laughing in a high, shrill animal voice. Letting the cold air rush at my burning face. My burning, ugly face.

I ran hard and fast. Ran like a wild creature, past the tall, silent trees and the dark houses.

Ran till I couldn't hear her unhappy cries anymore.

I had to stop to catch my breath. Where was I? I didn't recognize the houses. The moon was still behind the clouds. Darkness covered the street signs.

*Got to get control.*

*Got to do an act of kindness before I completely disappear and become this evil creature forever.*

Up ahead, I heard a car door slam. I turned and saw a young man standing beside a small SUV. He was shaking his head and muttering under his breath.

I took a few steps toward him. As I came closer, I saw that he was staring down at a flat tire. Angrily, he slammed his fist on the car hood.

I walked closer. He gasped when he saw me. My face must have scared him.

"That's a really frightening mask," he said. "You startled me."

"Happy Halloween," I grunted.

"Not too happy for me," he said. "I'm miles from home and look." He pointed to the flat tire.

I nodded. What did he want me to say?

He waved a cell phone in front of me. "My phone is out of power. I can't call anyone to come change the tire." He squinted at me. "Do you have a phone I can use?"

I shrugged. "Sorry."

"Hey, how old are you? Aren't you out awfully late by yourself?"

Why was this guy asking me so many questions? The anger started to build up inside me.

*Stay calm. Stay in control.*

"I'm going to a party," I lied in my raspy voice. "A few blocks from here. My parents know where I am."

He thought for a moment. "Would you do me a big favor?"

"Do you mean an act of kindness?" I asked.

That made him laugh. "Yeah, I guess. Could you stay here and watch my car? I've got a lot of valuable things in the trunk."

"Stay here?" I said.

"Just for a minute or two. I'm going to run over to those houses over there and see if anyone will let me use their phone. I can't lock the car. The locks are broken."

"No problem," I grunted. "I'll wait here. It's an act of kindness, right?"

He nodded. "Yes. Thank you." He squinted at me. "Isn't that mask really *tight*?"

"It's okay," I said. "Really."

"Okay. Be right back." He took off running. I spotted a house with its lights on about half a block away.

I leaned my back against the SUV. I shut my eyes.

*I'm doing an act of kindness.*

If only I could fight off the evil power from the mask. The evil power that invaded my mind. I could feel it now, waves of evil, red-hot anger, muscle-gripping fury.

I gritted my teeth. I tightened every muscle in my body. I concentrated ... concentrated on pushing back my evil thoughts.

But ...

*"Here's an act of kindness!"* I howled.

I bent down and gripped the flat tire in both hands. Then with all the strength of my unspeakable anger, I *ripped* the tire off the car!

I heaved the tire into the street. It bounced to the other curb.

Then I tossed back my head and laughed. I couldn't keep the horrible laughter inside me.

I could feel the blood pulsing in my veins now. Pulsing in my head. Throbbing like a crazy drumbeat.

I leaned over the rear tire, grabbed it — and ripped it off the car. I heaved it beside the other one.

Panting like an animal, I moved to the other side of the car. I pulled the other two tires off and slammed them to the ground.

I turned and saw the young man returning, walking slowly down a driveway.

Wiping my hands on the sides of my costume, I turned again and bolted away.

I heard him call to me, but I didn't look back. I ducked my head and ran into the late-night breeze. Ran to darkness.

Darkness.

Where I belonged.

*How can I do an act of kindness when the evil of the mask overpowers me each time?*

*Is there a way to trick it?*

I stopped when I recognized the house across the street from me. Polly's house. The lights still on. The living-room window glass shattered, glittering shards on the lawn.

Polly's house. Where my night of horror had started.

And where it was about to continue.

"What are *you* doing here?"

Polly's mother dropped the vacuum cleaner hose and glared angrily at me.

Polly had a plastic garbage bag in her hand. She was collecting pieces of glass and lumps of food off the floor. She had changed into jeans and a gray sweatshirt.

The living room was still a horrible mess. The food table still lay on its side. The rug was stained and spotted with food and spilled drinks. It looked like a hurricane had blown through.

Hurricane Lu-Ann.

"Go away, Lu-Ann," Polly said through gritted teeth. "Why did you come back? You're not welcome here."

"I'll call the police," her mom said. "They were already here once. They couldn't believe the damage one girl could do." She sighed. "My insurance company won't believe it, either."

"You ruined my party," Polly said in a trembling voice. "We all . . . we all just wanted to have some fun. And you ruined it!"

They both narrowed their eyes and scowled at me.

"I . . . I'm so sorry," I murmured. "I came back to apologize. And to help clean up."

"We don't want your help," Polly's mom said.

"Why did you do it, Lu-Ann?" Polly asked.

"I . . . don't know," I answered. "I can't explain it."

"Do you *hate* me? I thought we were friends."

"I don't hate you, Polly," I said. "It's just . . ."

"Why do you still have that horrible mask on?" her mom demanded. "Take it off. It's not funny. It's making me sick. Really."

"I can't take it off!" The words burst out of me. "Don't you see?" I screamed. "It won't come off!"

"That's not funny," Polly said. "I thought you came back to help us. So why are you telling such a stupid lie?"

"It's not a lie," I said, trying to calm down. "Look at me, Polly. Look —"

Her mom let out a long sigh. "Just go home, Lu-Ann. You've done enough damage for one night."

She turned to the living-room window. Gusts of cold wind blew in through the open hole. "I can't get anyone out here this late to cover up the window. It's freezing in here. Look what you've done. Just look what you've done."

"I can help," I said.

She was right. I'd done a horrible thing. But she wasn't trying to understand. She didn't want to believe me about the mask. She said I was a liar.

*A liar . . . a liar . . . a liar . . .*

"I can help," I said. "Watch."

I picked up a long-handled broom. And I swung the handle into a table lamp. The lamp cracked and toppled off the table, shattering on the floor.

Then I swept the broom over the mantel, knocking all the little pumpkins to the floor. I walked over them and stomped hard on them, smashing their pumpkin goo into the carpet.

Then with my incredible evil strength, I *pushed* the tip of the broom handle into the back of the couch. It split the leather and slid

111

right through the couch, and poked out of the other side.

"*See how I can help?*" I screamed.

Polly and her mom were running around in frantic circles, shouting and wailing in a total panic.

"Go home, Lu-Ann! Go home! Go home! You're *sick*!" Polly shrieked, her face bright red, her eyes bulging in horror and disbelief.

Her mom grabbed the phone. I knew she was calling the police.

All I wanted to do was apologize and help them clean up the mess I'd made. But I couldn't control myself. The Haunted Mask was telling me what to do. Forcing me to do its evil.

I tipped over the coffee table. Then I picked up the vacuum cleaner cord and tore it in half.

Polly came charging at me and tried to tackle me. I spun away and darted to the stairs.

Breathing hard, I ran all the way up to the attic. The lamp was still on. The black-and-gold chest sat open near the wall. Costumes were strewn over the floor. The closet door was closed.

The closet . . .

Once again, I pictured the ghost inside the closet. The terrifying ghost that had grabbed me and tried to pull me inside.

Suddenly, I had a crazy idea.

I took a few steps toward the closet door, thinking hard.

That hideous old ghost . . . I never had a chance to warn Polly about him.

Maybe I could scare the ghost away. Maybe I could use the evil of the Haunted Mask to chase the ghost from the closet.

That would be an act of kindness for Polly and her mother, right? That would be an act of *unbelievable* kindness. The kind Marcus's dad was talking about.

My hand trembled as I reached for the closet door. But before I could pull it open, I heard a sound. I turned and saw Polly at the top of the steps.

She gazed around the long room until she found me. "Lu-Ann, hear those sirens?" she said. "Those are the police. Coming for you."

Yes. I could hear them. Very faint. Far away. But getting closer.

I didn't have much time. I squeezed the handle to the closet door.

Polly came running toward me. "What are you doing? Lu-Ann, get away from there. The police will be here in minutes. You can't hide in that closet."

"I . . . don't want to hide," I murmured. "I'm going to do you a big favor. There's a ghost —"

I tugged the closet door open.

Polly burst up beside me. "Get away. Get out of here."

"Wait," I said. "I —"

I didn't get to finish my sentence.

A bony hand shot out of the darkness of the closet and wrapped its skeletal fingers around Polly's shoulder.

"Huh?" A startled cry escaped her throat as a second hand grabbed on to her.

The old ghost appeared in the closet doorway with his cracked skull, patchy skin, and sunken eyes. "*So lonely . . .*" he groaned.

114

I saw him tighten his grip on Polly. Tighten it until she screamed.

"Help me! Oh, help! He's got me! He's pulling me! Help me! He's pulling me into the closet!"

And as I stared, frozen in horror, the disgusting old ghost gave a hard tug.

And Polly vanished into the darkness.

"Hahahahahaha!"

A burst of evil laughter escaped my throat. I tossed back my head and laughed.

*No, Lu-Ann. Fight the evil. Fight it.*

I clamped a hand over my mouth, struggled to hold in the laughter.

*Fight the evil, Lu-Ann.*

I forced myself to move. I lurched forward and stumbled into the closet. Blinking in the dark, I spotted the old man, now with his hands around Polly's waist, pulling her . . . dragging her deeper into the closet.

*"So loooooonely . . ."* he moaned.

"No way!" I shouted.

I wrapped my arms around Polly and pulled her free. Then I leaped at the old ghost. Tackled him around his bone-hard waist.

A squeak escaped his ragged throat. *"The mask . . . Nooo . . . The mask . . ."* He went down hard.

I heard the crack of bones. He let out a soft wisp of air. One leg cracked and split off his body. It came sliding out from his black pants leg.

I lifted myself off him. In time to see his head crack in two. It rolled off his bony neck. Rolled against the wall with the sunken eyes staring straight up.

He didn't move.

Polly stood with her hands wrapped around her chest. Shaking. Eyes rolling in her head.

I grabbed her gently and led her out of the closet, into the light of the attic. "You're okay," I whispered, smoothing her hair off her face. "Polly, you're okay now."

"Thank you, Lu-Ann," she said.

I grabbed at the mask over my face. I knew I had done it. Saving Polly from the ghost *had* to be an act of unbelievable kindness.

I tugged both sides up.

117

*Come off. Come OFF.*

I fumbled for the bottom of the mask. Struggled to lift it up. To slide the tight, hot mask up my face.

No.

Not happening.

*Please . . . please come off!*

Saving Polly wasn't enough. Or had Mr. Wright lied? Had he given me the wrong solution?

No. Why would he do that?

He was an expert on all kinds of masks. He would know how to remove the Haunted Mask.

I tried one more time. I tugged at it. I twisted it. I pinched it hard and pulled.

*Noooooo.*

The mask was my skin now. My skin. My hideous green skin.

The sirens grew very loud. The police were on Polly's block now. Seconds away.

I took off running. Down the two flights of stairs. Through the back hall and out the kitchen door.

I ran as fast as I could, the sirens blaring in my ears.

Faster . . . Faster . . .

I ran to the street. Ran past houses and yards. Ran till I saw only a stream of dark colors all around me. Ran under the cold glow of the Halloween moon.

Ran ... Ran ...

But to *where*?

Where could I go?

# PART THREE:

# DEVIN'S STORY

My three *least* favorite things in the world?

1. Soggy Oreo cookies.
2. Homework on any day of the week.
3. Walking in a pumpkin field at night.

So here I was, Devin O'Bannon, walking through an endless pumpkin field on a cold October night. No moon in the sky. And chilly gusts of wind that made the fat pumpkin leaves scrape and slap one another.

And just to make the moment perfect, my twin sisters, Dale and Dolly, both six, tagging along.

Pulling my hand, tugging me through the tangles of disgusting leaves and vines, tripping and singing, and laughing at their older, wiser brother — as always.

Did I wish I was back home, sitting on my friend Lu-Ann's couch, tossing down handfuls of popcorn and trading insults with her?

Three guesses.

But like I said, here I was, walking through the pumpkin field with my sisters. My Number Three least favorite thing to do. Mainly because pumpkins are so creepy. I mean, have you ever looked at pumpkin leaves?

They are big dudes. Fat and kind of round. They remind me of baseball gloves. They look like they're about to grab you and pull you and suck you inside them. You know. Like those snapping plants that like to eat flies.

And those fat, ugly leaves are noisy, too. When the wind comes up and they slap against one another, it sounds like hands clapping. Weird.

*Clap clap clap clap.* A whole field of hands clapping.

And you know why they're clapping? Because they've just grabbed some poor victim and sucked him inside the vine.

Okay, okay. Maybe that's not true. Dad says I have a runaway imagination. And that's what I'd like to do. Run away. Because this pumpkin farm is *creepy* with a capital C.

And I haven't even started to talk about the vines. They're mostly hidden beneath the fat, clapping leaves. That's so you can trip over them more easily.

Pumpkin vines are thick and long. Wider around than snakes. Really. That's exactly what they look like. Long, thick snakes with pumpkins growing at one end.

Yuck — right?

And that's not all that's scary about this farm. There's a huge black cat named Zeus who follows us everywhere. Zeus has the most evil stare I've ever seen. Talk about bad luck. He definitely has the Evil Eye.

And he follows me silently. Watching . . . always watching.

Then there's Mrs. Barnes. She's the housekeeper and cook who came with the farm. Mrs. Barnes is a big, round woman with long black braids that go all the way down her back. Like vines.

Her face is round and her body is round. As if she's *built* of pumpkins!

But I'm being unfair. She is actually very nice. She has a warm, friendly smile and a soft voice, and she gave me an extra stack of pancakes this morning, which were great.

But not great enough — because here I was on this cold October night a week before Halloween, walking with my sisters in this endless field of pumpkins.

"This is so *awesome!*" Dolly exclaimed. She did a little dance on the soft, mushy ground.

It's such a pain to have a sister who is wrong all the time.

It's an even bigger pain to have *two* sisters who are always wrong.

But they're both cute as they come, with ringlets of blond hair and big blue eyes, giggly laughs, little turned-up noses, and dimples in their chins.

Dad calls them little leprechauns.

Leprechauns come from Ireland, where he was born. And he means it as a compliment. But I looked up leprechauns online, and it said they were little creatures who do a lot of mischief.

Dolly and Dale started dancing around a big pumpkin, singing some dumb Halloween song. Dale grabbed me and tried to pull me into their circle to do the dance with them.

Like that was really going to happen.

Let's be honest. I was totally creeped out in this field. I mean, it was very dark and there could be hundreds of *real* snakes slithering along the snaky vines. And all kinds of other creatures.

I mean, this field was a *horror movie* waiting to happen.

But I had to act brave for the girls. I'm the older brother and that's my job, right?

I tugged free of them and took a few steps back. The fat leaves brushed the legs of my jeans. That sent chills up my spine.

And in the darkness, I suddenly saw two glowing green eyes. Cat eyes. Zeus had followed us again.

The girls were dancing faster and faster, circling the big pumpkin and singing:

*"Jack Jack Jack-o'-lantern*
*Jack-o'-lantern come ALIVE!*
*Come alive! Come alive!*
*Jack Jack Jack Jack."*

"Come alive? Are you kidding me?" I shouted over their shrill little singing voices.

They both laughed.

"Where did you learn that song?" I asked.

"We made it up, stupid," Dolly replied.

"Yes, we make up songs all the time," Dale said. "Why won't you dance with us, Devin? Don't you think it's cool to dance in the dark like this?"

127

"Not cool," I said. "Totally not cool. Let's go back to the house. It's getting cold."

"No, it isn't."

See? I'm always wrong.

*"Jack Jack Jack-o'-lantern*
*Jack-o'-lantern come ALIVE!*
*Come alive! Come alive!*
*Jack Jack Jack Jack."*

"Stop singing that!" I shouted. Their dumb song was giving me the creeps, too. I was shivering. Really.

Hey, I'm a city guy. I grew up in New York City. My first seven years, at least. Before we moved to Dayton, Ohio. I don't belong on a farm.

I can't believe Dad leased this pick-your-own-pumpkin farm. But he lost his job last year. And he's been scrambling around, trying to find ways to make money ever since.

So, I try not to complain. I only tell him how much I hate it here five or ten times a day.

A strong gust of wind came blowing down the length of the field. The trees near the fence bent and made weird groaning sounds. The pumpkin leaves rattled and shook at my feet.

"I . . . I'm going inside," I said to the twins. "Are you coming?"

I didn't wait for their answer. I turned and started to jog toward the house, jumping over the long, fat vines.

"WHOOOOAAAA!"

I tripped over a vine.

Nothing to grab on to. Nothing to stop myself from falling.

I saw the glowing cat eyes watching me as I went down.

I landed with a thud. My head hit something hard. A pumpkin? A rock?

My knees throbbed. Pain shot up and down my body.

Everything went black. Blacker than the night sky.

I fought it. I forced my eyes to open. Pain danced around my head, circling me. I could feel the blood pulsing at my temples.

"Ohhhhh." A low moan escaped my throat. I shook my head hard, trying to shake away the pain.

"Are you okay?"

"Devin, are you hurt?"

My twin sisters leaned over me, staring down with wide eyes.

"No. Not okay," I said. I held my hands out and let them pull me to a sitting position.

"What's wrong?" Dolly asked.

"Didn't you *see* what happened?" I cried.

They both shook their heads. "You tripped?" Dale said.

"No," I said. "Didn't you see that vine move? That vine right there." I pointed to it. "It moved. It *tripped* me. Really. I saw it move!"

# 2

The girls just laughed. They thought I was joking, but I wasn't.

Squinting into the darkness, I could swear I saw the vines crawling over the ground, twisting, tangling over one another as they stretched and slithered.

I stood up and rubbed my head. I could feel a bump on my forehead from where I hit. No blood. But I knew I'd have an ugly bruise.

The cool wind felt good on my hot face. Except for the clapping of the leaves, the pumpkin field was silent. No night birds. The crickets of summer were all gone.

"Come on. Into the house," I said. "Enough thrills and chills for one night."

That's when a long creature rose up in front of me and attacked my face.

"Snake! Snake!" Dolly shrieked.

I screamed.

The girls burst out laughing. Dale waved the vine in my face. She had it gripped in both hands.

I should have known she was moving the vine. But I was freaked from my fall.

"You two are about as funny as moldy pumpkin guts," I said.

That made them laugh even harder. Okay. Fine. Let them enjoy their joke.

I didn't feel like laughing. I was pretty miserable.

I mean, I had to spend a whole week on this farm. A whole week of caring for the pumpkins, and hauling them to peoples' cars, and helping guide the visitors, and working the cash register, and just general farm work.

A whole week away from school and my friends.

As soon as we came inside, I phoned Lu-Ann to see how she was doing back in our neighborhood.

"I'm still dreading Polly Martin's party," she said. "It's going to be so lame. Brad and Marcus and I are thinking hard. But we can't come up with any good ideas to help make the party exciting."

"I know what you can do," I said, rubbing the bump on my forehead. "You can come here. There's plenty of extra rooms. And you can do all of *my* jobs! Fun, right?"

She didn't laugh. "You know I can't come there, Devin. No way my parents would let me miss school so I can go pick pumpkins on your farm."

"But, Lu-Ann," I said, "this farm is less than an hour from your house. Maybe you could —"

"Forget it, Devin. No way. Not happening." She shouted something to her mom. I heard them talking for a minute.

Then she came back to the phone. "Are you hating it there?"

"*Hating* isn't the right word," I said. "I think maybe *despising* is the perfect word." Lu-Ann and I are always looking for perfect words.

"Well, when you start to feel bad, just think about how lucky you are to be missing Polly's party."

I started to answer, but something caught my eye. A reflection in my bedroom window. Something bright and fiery.

I stared hard at the reflection in the window. It took me a few seconds to realize it was a large jack-o'-lantern. The reflection of a flaming, grinning jack-o'-lantern. Floating inside my room!

I let out a shocked cry. I spun around.

Nothing in my room. No jack-o'-lantern. No floating pumpkin.

I turned back to the window. And saw the grinning pumpkin in the glass. It flickered brightly. A reflection from my room.

I spun around again. No jack-o'-lantern in the room.

Then, as I turned my eyes to the window, I saw the pumpkin slowly fade in the dark glass. It faded to nothing. Disappeared as I stared, my heart pounding.

Whoa.

*How can there be a reflection of something that isn't here?*

"Devin? Devin? What's wrong? Why did you scream?"

I heard Lu-Ann's alarmed voice in my phone.

"I . . . I've got to go," I said. I kept my eyes on the window. Black as the night now.

"But are you okay?"

"Yeah. I guess. Later," I said. I clicked the phone off and tossed it onto my bed. Then I bolted out of my room. Ran down the hall and out the back door.

A burst of freezing wind blew me back. But I ran to the side of the house, my eyes searching the darkness for the bright jack-o'-lantern.

No. Not out here.

Not in my room. And not outside. But I didn't imagine it. No way I imagined it.

I rubbed the bump on my head. It hurt a lot.

Was it causing me to *see* things?

*Hallucinate.* That's a perfect word.

"Anyone out here?" I called. My voice sounded strangely hollow in the heavy night air.

Silence. Except for the clatter of the pumpkin leaves. And the scrape . . . the *scrape . . . scrape . . . scrape* of the long vines as they crawled over the soft dirt.

No. Wait.

Why were the vines making that sound? That wasn't normal — was it?

Wrapping my arms around myself to keep warm, I took a few steps away from the back of the house. I stepped out of the light from my bedroom window and moved toward the pumpkin field.

It took a while for my eyes to adjust to the blackness. It was so dark, I couldn't see where the sky ended and the ground began.

But as I moved closer, I could hear the slither of the vines clearly. Yes. I could hear them stretching . . . stretching . . .

The vines were moving. *Dozens of them.*

Crawling toward the house, dragging the pumpkins with them.

I realized I wasn't breathing. I'd been holding my breath. I let it out in a long whoosh. My breath steamed in front of me.

And as the steam floated away, my eyes focused on some pumpkins on the ground. Large, round pumpkins right in front of me.

I gasped when I saw them moving. Their sides moved in, then out. Tiny movements. But I could see them.

In, then out.

They were breathing.

The pumpkins were breathing.

"Nooooo." A low moan escaped my throat. My whole body shook with fright.

I turned and ran. My shoes slid on the loose dirt as I bolted back into the house. I burst down the hall and into my parents' room.

I know. I was supposed to knock. But I was too frightened to remember anything. I just lowered my shoulder and pushed the door open.

They were sound asleep under the covers in their bed. "Mom! Dad!" I ran to the bed and shook them awake.

"Huh? What?" Mom blinked her eyes in confusion.

"Devin? What's wrong?" Dad's voice was clogged with sleep.

"It's . . . the vines," I choked out. I was panting so hard I could barely speak. "They're growing. They're moving. I saw them. You've got to believe me. The vines are crawling like snakes. Crawling to the house. And the pumpkins — I saw them *breathing*!"

"Yes, I know," Dad said, raising his head from the pillow. "I meant to tell you about that."

"Huh?" I stared at Dad, my heart pounding.

"Devin," Dad said, "we also hired two dozen monkeys to sit on the pumpkins and keep them from hopping away."

Mom and Dad both burst out laughing.

I stood there with my mouth hanging open. I waited for them to stop. "Uh . . . does this mean you don't believe me?"

That made them start laughing again.

"No, we don't believe you," Mom said. She reached out and grabbed my hand. Her hand was very warm. Mine was frozen.

"We don't believe the vines were crawling or the pumpkins were breathing," Mom said. "We know you don't want to be here, kiddo. But making up scary stories won't help you get home."

"I — I didn't make it up."

She squeezed my hand. "Go back to bed, Devin. You were having one of your bad dreams." She tucked her hand back under the covers.

I turned and started to the bedroom door. "Sorry I woke you up."

I was pretty sure it wasn't a bad dream. It's true I have a lot of nightmares. And yes, they are very real. And I remember them all after I wake up. And sometimes I get confused and think they really happened. But not for long.

And this time I knew it couldn't be a nightmare. Because I wasn't asleep. When I saw the reflection of the jack-o'-lantern, I was talking to Lu-Ann on the phone.

I was finally starting to breathe normally. I walked down the hall to my room. This was an old farmhouse, and the floorboards all creaked as I walked.

The house groaned and cracked and made weird noises all the time. And the old radiators hissed and rattled when the heat came up.

*Like a haunted house.*

I scolded myself for thinking like that. "Come on, Devin. You're only going to be living here for a week. What could happen in a week?"

I heard my sisters giggling in their room. It was nearly midnight and they were still awake. They were so excited about living on this farm and in this creaky old house, they could barely sit still. And they stayed up till all hours making up pumpkin games and songs.

Why couldn't I enjoy it like them?

Pumpkins don't breathe. And vines don't slither like snakes.

Why did I have to imagine these things?

*Just relax, Devin.*

"Ohh!" I uttered a cry as a large figure stepped into the dim hall.

It took me a few seconds to recognize Mrs. Barnes. She stepped toward me with a smile on her round face. Her long braids fell down the back of her heavy gray nightgown.

"Trouble sleeping, Devin?" Her silvery eyes studied me.

"Uh . . . kinda," I said.

"You're probably just excited. Farm life is more exciting than people think."

"Exciting?" I said.

She nodded. "All the creatures in the outdoors

and things growing everywhere. It's a world apart from city life."

"You got that right," I muttered.

"I have just the thing for you," she said, motioning with one finger for me to follow her. "A nice hot cup of pumpkin tea."

*Huh?*

"Pumpkin tea?" My stomach did a quick flip-flop.

"Just the thing to relax you, dearie." Her silvery eyes didn't blink. I knew she was trying to be nice. But she was starting to freak me out.

"Uh . . . no thanks," I said. "I'm fine."

Her face fell. She looked disappointed. I said good night, stepped into my room, and closed the door behind me.

*Pumpkin tea?*

A few seconds later, I climbed into bed and pulled the covers up. The bedroom window rattled, and I felt a cold wind blowing over the room.

I shut my eyes and tried not to think about the farm. Instead, I thought about Polly Martin's Halloween party, and Lu-Ann and my friends scheming to make it more exciting.

I opened my eyes and gazed into the darkness. It took a while but I finally started to feel sleepy.

Yes. I was about to fall asleep. My eyelids felt heavy . . . heavy . . .

The last thing I saw was an orange glow on the bedroom window glass.

Next morning, bright sunlight poured into the bedroom window. It warmed my face and woke me up. I sat up straight, instantly alert.

During the night, I had a bad dream about scarecrows. Scarecrows in my house. No, wait. In the dream, my mom and dad and two sisters — they were chasing me through a farm field. And as they ran, they all turned into scarecrows.

Crazy.

I yawned loudly. I stretched my hands high above my head.

The sunlight felt nice on my face. *Today is going to be better*, I told myself.

*Today I'm putting on my new face. A whole new attitude. I'm going to be like my sisters. I'm going to make the most of my two weeks here. I'm going to have FUN.*

I had a smile on my face as I turned, pushed back the covers, and lowered my feet to the floor.

"Aaaaack."

I expected to feel the hard floorboards. But instead, my bare feet sank into something warm and squishy.

142

I jerked my feet up in surprise. "Oh, yuck!"

They were covered in some kind of drippy orange-yellow goo.

Slowly, I peered down.

"Oh, wow."

Leaning forward, I saw the round puddle of orange glop on the floor beside my bed. I quickly recognized the sour smell.

Pumpkin meat. Pulpy, sticky pumpkin meat.

I was staring down at a pile of it, a huge puddle of pumpkin guts.

*How did it get there?*

Someone dropped the puddle of pumpkin guts beside my bed. But who?

It had to be a joke, a mean joke. Someone knew I would step in it and be totally grossed out.

Dale and Dolly didn't do this, I decided. It just wasn't their style. Their jokes were silly — not mean and disgusting.

Someone had sneaked into my room during the night and left that pile of gunk there. Who in this house would do such a thing?

I couldn't help it. I left orange, pulpy footprints across the floor as I walked to the bathroom. I took an extra-long shower, and washed my feet at least five times.

I was still thinking about the pumpkin guts as I made my way to the kitchen. The house has a big farmhouse kitchen with a fireplace on one wall, a long wooden table like a picnic table, and a super-sized stove and fridge.

Dale and Dolly were already at the table, spooning up big bowls of cereal. Mrs. Barnes turned from the sink and smiled at me. "Did you finally get to sleep, Devin?"

I nodded. "Yes. No problem."

"I'm making you a big plate of scrambled eggs and bacon this morning," she said. "You work up a big appetite on a farm."

"Cool," I said. I studied the twins. They were splashing milk on each other. Eating each other's Corn Flakes.

I knew they weren't the pumpkin-goo culprits.

Zeus hunched in front of the fireplace, watching us eat. He was the biggest cat I'd ever seen. Bigger than our old cocker spaniel. The cat never made a sound. Just watched us and followed us silently.

After breakfast, Dad led Dale, Dolly, and me out back to a wooden shed. He pointed to a pile of small pumpkins on the ground in front of a low bench.

"I brought these little pumpkins here for you to paint," he said. He pointed to a small table with jars of red, black, and white paint. "Paint funny faces on them. You know. Some creepy ones. Some grinning ones. Some cute faces."

I picked up a little pumpkin and rolled it around in my hand. "And why are we doing this?" I asked.

"People like to buy ready-made jack-o'-lanterns," Dad said. "You know. Pumpkins they don't have to carve."

"I get it," I said.

The girls were already sitting on the bench, opening jars of paint.

"Go wild. Paint the funniest faces you can," Dad said. "We'll sell them for ten dollars each."

Dolly dipped a paintbrush in a jar of red paint. Then she raised the brush to Dale's face. Dale tried to squirm away.

"Hold still," Dolly said. "I'm painting you cool red lips."

"Stop right there," Dad said. He grabbed Dolly's wrist and pulled her hand away from Dale. "Don't paint each other. You already have funny faces!"

"Ha-ha," Dolly said. "You're so funny." She pulled her hand free and smeared a red stripe on Dad's forehead.

He laughed. He thinks everything the twins do is hilarious. "Paint the pumpkins," he told them. "Be serious. I mean it. This is work. Not play."

He headed back to the house.

The girls placed pumpkins in their laps and concentrated on painting them. Dale moved her brush in circles, making big black eyes on her pumpkin. Dolly painted the whole front of her pumpkin white. Then she started to add red eyes on the white background.

"Nice work," I said. "You two are good face painters."

"Can I paint *your* face?" Dolly asked. She poked her brush at me.

I scooted away. "You heard what Dad said. We have to be serious. This is work."

"Look. I'm almost finished with mine, and you haven't even started," Dale said.

"Okay, okay." I picked up a small yellowish pumpkin and smoothed the dirt off it with my hand. "I'm going to make all my pumpkins look just like you two," I said.

Dolly held hers up in front of me. "This one already looks like you, Devin," she said. "See? It's yellow and wrinkled and gross?"

"Let's see who can paint the funniest one," I said.

I had the little pumpkin in one hand. I reached for a paintbrush — then stopped.

"Hey!" I let out a cry when I heard the sound. Like a low groan. Coming from the pumpkin!

Suddenly, the hard pumpkin skin turned *soft*. Soft as human skin!

"Devin, what's your problem?" The twins were staring at me.

"It . . . it's the pumpkin," I stammered. "It feels soft — like a human face. And I heard it *burp* or something! Look. It's ALIVE!"

The girls just stared at me.

I heard it again. A soft groan.

With a startled gasp, I jumped to my feet. I dropped the pumpkin. I bumped the table. It toppled over — and all the paint jars went tumbling to the ground.

Red, black, and white paint spread in wide puddles at our feet.

The girls jumped up and danced over the spilled paint. "You ruined everything!" Dale shouted angrily.

"We were having fun," Dolly said. "You spoiled it."

"What's going on here?" Dad appeared, jogging across the backyard toward us. "What happened to the paint?" Of course, he had his eyes on me.

"I'm sorry, Dad," I said. "But . . . the pumpkin . . . I picked up a pumpkin and its skin got soft and it made weird noises and it felt like a human face, not like a pumpkin."

The words all burst out in a whoosh. I didn't take a breath.

"Which pumpkin?" Dad asked.

I pointed. The pumpkin sat on the ground at the edge of the puddle of red paint.

Dad bent down and picked up the pumpkin. He tapped it with a finger. He squeezed it. "It's hard, Devin. It feels like a pumpkin."

"But, Dad —"

He squeezed it again. "Not making any sounds, is it?"

"No," I said, shaking my head. "I'm really sorry. But —"

"Devin, come here," Dad said softly. He put a hand around the back of my neck and guided me gently around to the other side of the shed. "Devin, let's have a talk."

"You mean our usual man-to-man talk where you tell me I'm acting like a jerk?"

"Yes," he said. "That talk."

"I'm totally sorry about the paint," I said. "But the pumpkin really did feel weird. And —"

"Devin, I know you didn't want to do this farm thing. I know you're unhappy about it. But your bad attitude is going to spoil it for everyone else. I need you to pitch in and help out. The girls need you to look after them and guide them. Not scare them and ruin their projects."

"I know, but —"

"Do you think you can just shape up? It's only for such a short time."

"Sure, Dad," I said. "No problem. I'm going to try a lot harder. I promise." I raised my right hand like I was swearing an oath.

I was being sincere. I really did feel bad. I didn't want to be the one to mess up all the time.

*If I see something weird, I'm going to ignore it.*

*I'm going to be a happy camper for the rest of the time here.*

I followed Dad back around to the side of the shed. Mrs. Barnes had helped the girls set the table back up with fresh paint jars.

The three of us started to paint faces on the little pumpkins again. The twins were really good at it. They painted some crazy, goofy faces. I painted angry, scary faces, mostly black-and-white.

As we painted, the girls started singing their jack-o'-lantern song again:

*"Jack Jack Jack-o'-lantern*
*Jack-o'-lantern come ALIVE!"*

I hate that song.

I begged them to stop. Guess what? That made them sing the thing even louder.

I was so happy when Mom came out and took the girls away. She was going to drive them into town to do some shopping.

I counted about twelve pumpkins to go. I put my serious face on and got into it. I wanted to see how many different expressions I could paint.

I've always liked Art class. Our Art teacher says I'm a little bit talented. I can draw really well. In fifth grade, I did a few watercolors that are now hanging in the hall at school.

I had my head down, concentrating on a really sad white face, when it suddenly grew dark around me.

A shadow fell over me. A heavy shadow.

I looked up — and saw a boy standing over me. A boy in jeans and a white T-shirt — *and a big, round pumpkin on his shoulders instead of a head!*

"Huh?" I let out a gasp.

I gaped up at the pumpkin head. How was it attached to the boy's shoulders?

I suddenly knew I was in a horror movie. *Invasion of the Pumpkin Heads!*

But then the pumpkin began to slide down. I realized the boy was holding it in both hands. Holding it in front of his face.

*Whew. I really am starting to go crazy on this farm.*

He was pale and very skinny. His jeans sort of hung on him. He had straight brown hair that fell over his forehead. Dark eyes, a serious expression, even though he was giving me a lop-sided smile.

I set down the pumpkin I was painting and jumped up. "Hi," I said. "You . . . star-tled me."

"Sorry." He had a soft voice, whispery, like he had a sore throat. He pointed to the big pumpkin he'd been carrying.

"This pumpkin . . . it's too perfect. So I picked it. I'm going to give it to my mom."

I blinked. "Your mom?"

He nodded. He brushed the long hair off his forehead, but it flopped right back down over his dark eyes.

"I'm Haywood Barnes," he said. "You know. Mrs. Barnes's son."

"Oh, hi," I said. "I . . . didn't know. I'm Devin O'Bannon."

"I know," he replied. He gave me that same lopsided smile. One side of his mouth moved up higher than the other side.

"My mom talked to your dad. I'm going to help out with the pumpkins and everything. You know. Help carry them and pick them, and help with the customers when they come."

"Nice," I said. "Hey, I'm stoked to have some help. I don't really know anything about this farm stuff."

He dropped down beside me on the bench. We chatted for a while. I told him a little about my family and why we were here on the pumpkin farm this Halloween.

He kept rubbing the knees of his jeans as we talked. I noticed that his hands were long and very pale.

He told me about all the weird pumpkin recipes his mom had. It made him laugh. He said she could make *anything* out of pumpkin meat. But it all tasted exactly the same.

We talked about roasted pumpkin seeds. I confessed I'd never tried them.

"It's the best," he said. "Better than popcorn. Really. You just drop them in oil and cook them on the stove. The best!"

In front of us, two large blackbirds had a fight over a long green insect. They were really going at it. It made us both laugh.

I liked this guy. He was fun to talk to. It was great to have someone about my age to hang with.

Zeus crept out of the tall grass. The cat spotted the blackbirds. He arched his back. I could see his fur stand up. He lowered his head and started to stalk them, moving in slow motion.

The birds saw him. Squawking and flapping, they took off and flew away before the cat made his move.

Haywood snickered. "Lots of drama on this farm."

"Where do you live?" I asked.

He pointed toward the fields. "Off that way. Not far."

"Your mom lives with us in the farmhouse," I said.

"Yeah. And I live with my dad and a bunch of other people."

I saw my dad heading into the garage. "Did you meet my dad? There he is." I pointed.

Haywood jumped up. "I'll go say hi. Catch you later." He took off running.

I picked up the pumpkin I was painting. Only a few more to go. Dad would be happy.

I leaned forward to get a paintbrush — and glimpsed the pile of pumpkins my two sisters had painted. "Whoa. Wait a minute. *No way!*"

I stared at the faces painted on the pumpkins. Ugly monster faces. Some had evil red eyes. Green gobs of drool dripping from jagged-toothed mouths. Some had painted cracks down the middle of their faces. Fangs. One eye gouged out. Demon horns poking up from the top. One pumpkin appeared to have orange vomit pouring from its nostrils and open mouth.

*My sisters didn't paint these ugly faces!*

I jumped to my feet. I fumbled through the pumpkins, picking up each one, studying every face. All of them hideous. All of them disgusting. Totally gross.

I swore I would ignore anything weird that happened. But this was *too* weird. And this time I had *proof.*

I gathered them up. I stuffed as many of the ugly pumpkins as I could in my arms.

Holding them against my chest, I went running to the garage.

"Dad! Dad!" I screamed breathlessly. "Dad! Look at these! I *told* you something weird was happening on this farm! Dad — I've got *proof*!"

"Dad! I've got proof! Come look at this. Something is very wrong here! Dad!"

He was bent over a workbench, examining a pair of hedge clippers. I didn't see Haywood. I guessed he had gone home.

Dad turned as I came screaming into the garage. "Devin? What's up this time?"

"I've got proof!" I cried. "I told you something is weird here. Look at these pumpkins, Dad. Look at them."

I tried to hand them over to him. But they fell out of my arms and tumbled to the garage floor.

"Oh. Sorry."

Shaking his head, Dad dropped down on his knees and began gathering them up.

"See?" I cried. "Look at them."

"What about them?" he demanded.

"Dale and Dolly didn't paint those," I said.

He raised pumpkin after pumpkin and studied the painted faces. "Why not?" he asked.

"Huh?" I squatted down beside him.

He turned two pumpkins toward me. Cute smiley faces.

He set those down and picked up two more. Cross-eyed faces with goofy red tongues hanging out of grinning mouths.

"But — but —" I sputtered.

"These are cute," Dad said. "Your sisters did a good job." He narrowed his eyes at me. "What were you yelling about?"

"Well . . ."

Dad shook his head and frowned. "Devin, you promised me. You promised me you would try harder. And now you come running in here screaming about these cute little pumpkins?"

"But, Dad — they *weren't* cute. They —"

Dad tossed a smiley-face pumpkin into my hands. "I'm warning you, boy," he said.

He only calls me *boy* when he is angry.

"One more crazy stunt, and you'll be grounded for a *month* after we get home. And no cell-phone privileges for a month. I mean it."

"No phone? Dad, that's like cutting off my *oxygen!*"

I thought that would make him laugh, but it didn't. He climbed to his feet, picked up the hedge clippers, and stomped out of the garage.

I didn't move. I was still squatting down next to the cute little pumpkins. My brain was doing flip-flops.

If I could only figure out why all this weird stuff was happening to me.

I knew I had to be careful. Dad would be watching my every move now. Waiting for me to mess up.

He's not a very strict parent. And he's not mean at all. But once you get on his bad side, *look out!*

I suddenly had the feeling I wasn't alone. The back of my neck tingled. I felt someone was watching me.

Haywood?

No.

I turned and saw the big black cat hunched in the garage doorway. Staring at me. Not moving a whisker. The cat just stared with those cold green eyes.

"Zeus, what's your problem?" I called.

The cat didn't move.

I felt something bump against my knee.

Then several soft thuds.

I glanced down — and let out a shocked cry.

The little pumpkins — they were bouncing up and down. Bouncing like tennis balls on the concrete floor.

*Thud thud thud thud.*

"No way!" I cried, jumping to my feet.

The pumpkins all bounced together. Jumped in a circle around me. Their painted faces all grinned up at me.

As I stared, the faces turned ugly. The eyes darkened to red. The painted mouths opened and closed, making an eerie *bub bub bub* sound. One pumpkin began to vomit loudly. Thick orange goo poured from its open mouth. And then, *all* the pumpkins were vomiting, puking up yellow-orange lumps.

"Sick!" I screamed. "This is totally sick!"

My words made them start to laugh. Cold laughter. They circled me, faster and faster, their ugly laughter ringing in my head.

Trembling in fear, I covered my ears, burst through the circle, and ran for the house.

The day before Halloween, a gray, foggy Saturday, we opened the farm early. We knew it would be our busiest day.

Sure enough, cars and vans and SUVs began pulling into the parking lot. Families piled out, with lots of little kids, eager to explore the long, leafy fields and pick their own pumpkins.

My job was to sit in the shed near the entrance and work the cash register. It cost a five-dollar admission fee for each family. I collected the money and passed out tickets from an orange ticket roll Dad had bought from a movie theater in town.

Then when people made their pumpkin choices, they came back to my little wooden shed, and I rang up the sale.

I was happy to be in my little shed. The pumpkins definitely creeped me out. And I was grateful I didn't have to work in the fields.

Besides, it was a gray day with dark clouds hanging overhead. It looked like it might rain at any moment. I'd stay nice and dry under the flat shed roof.

Mom had a little stand near the entrance shed. That's where we had the pumpkins with the painted faces. She also had jars of pumpkin butter for sale, made by Mrs. Barnes. And a few pumpkin pies fresh from the oven.

The smell of the pies kept floating over to me, making me hungry. But I knew I wasn't allowed to leave the shed until someone came to take my place.

Dale and Dolly were the most excited people on the farm. Big surprise, right? They both wore orange skirts and black T-shirts with grinning jack-o'-lanterns on the front.

Dad told them they were the Official O'Bannon Farm Greeters. They stood side by side at the

163

edge of the field and shouted, "Hi! How are you today?" to everyone who passed by them.

They loved the job and didn't get tired of it. And everyone who saw them thought they were the cutest, most adorable things.

A lot of people stopped to talk to them. "Are you really twins?" a little girl asked. That made my sisters laugh. I mean, what *else* would they be?

Some people even stopped to have their picture taken with the girls.

That made me groan. I knew that after all the fuss and attention, Dolly and Dale would be *impossible* to live with.

*They are going to think they are STARS!*

Dad and Haywood worked the field. They guided people down the long vines, making a path through the thick, fat leaves. They helped people decide which pumpkins to pick.

Sometimes they had to cut the pumpkins off the vines. Then they helped carry the pumpkins to my booth, where I rang them up on the cash register.

Some families bought a lot of pumpkins. Some bought just one. They all seemed to love the idea of walking through the field and picking their own.

By late afternoon, the cash register was bulging with money. And the cars kept pulling in.

*Maybe this was a good idea,* I thought. *Maybe Dad was smart, after all.*

If only the rain would hold off. The sky was nearly as dark as night. And I felt a few cold raindrops blow onto my face through the open front of the shed.

A mom and dad with a tiny little boy stepped up in front of me. The dad set a big, weird-shaped pumpkin down on the counter. "One side is flat," he said. "Do I get a discount for that?"

I gazed at the pumpkin. It looked perfectly fine to me.

Dad said not to argue with the customers. "How about one dollar off?" I said.

That seemed to make him happy. The man pulled out his wallet and paid. Then the three of them headed to their car.

*Why did he pick a pumpkin with a flat side?* I wondered. *I mean, it was his choice.*

I didn't have long to think about it.

I slid the man's money into the cash register and was about to close the drawer — when I heard a shrill shout.

"Help! Help us!"

I recognized Dolly's voice.

"Someone! Help us! The pumpkins are alive!"

"They're alive!" Dale cried, screaming in fright.

"Help! The pumpkins are ALIVE!"

*Oh, wow.* "I knew it!" I muttered. "I *knew* it!"

I slammed the cash register drawer shut, leaped over the counter, and ran to help my sisters.

# 10

"Dolly? Dale?" I frantically screamed their names. "Are you okay?"

As I searched in a panic, it started to rain a little harder. I could hear the raindrops pattering on the pumpkin leaves. A light mist had settled over the field. People were hurrying to their cars.

I spotted the twins at the edge of the field. They were standing behind a row of three large pumpkins. All around them, the fat leaves trembled from the wind and sudden rain.

"What's wrong?" I cried breathlessly. I ran up

to them, my eyes on the pumpkins. "What's happening?"

The girls both burst out laughing.

"The pumpkins —" I said. "What happened? What did you see?"

"It was a joke," Dale said. She and Dolly bumped knuckles.

"We knew you'd believe us," Dolly said. "Because you're crazy."

All a joke. And I fell for it.

It made me angry. I don't like being fooled by two little squirts.

"Who says I'm crazy?" I barked.

"Dad says," Dale answered. They both had big grins on their faces.

"Dad says I'm crazy? I don't believe you."

"It's true," Dolly said. "He says ever since you got to this farm, you've been acting like you're nuts."

"*What* did I say?" Dad stepped between us. "Who is nuts?"

"Nothing," Dolly said. "Nobody."

"We were just teasing Devin," Dale told him.

"Well, why don't you tease him out of the rain?" Dad said. "It's starting to come down hard. Go. Go with your mother." He motioned to Mom, who was busy collecting everything off her table and putting them in a red wagon.

Dad turned to me. He slapped my shoulder. "We had a good day. Good work, Devin."

I followed him to the cash register. He removed the money drawer, turned, and motioned toward the farmhouse. "Are you coming?"

"In a second," I said. I saw Haywood standing under a tree. He held a black umbrella over his head. He seemed to be watching me.

I watched Mom, Dad, and the twins hurry down the path to the farmhouse. Behind me, the pumpkin leaves clattered and shook, pattered by the rain.

Pumpkins appeared to glow in the eerie yellow-gray light. Outside the field, the tall trees bent and swayed.

*It's like everything is strange. Nothing is normal.*

I trotted over to Haywood. He moved the umbrella so I could get under it, too.

"Don't know where this rain came from," he said. "The day started out so nice." He had a line of dirt down one side of his face. He was drenched in sweat, and his stringy hair fell over one eye.

"You worked hard," I said. "I had the easy job."

He snickered. "Maybe you want to trade?"

"I don't think so," I said, and I laughed.

He motioned to the field. "Still a lot of pumpkins

169

left for Halloween tomorrow. Your dad said it might be even more crowded than today."

The wind made a howling sound through the trees. The pumpkin leaves shook hard, slapping loudly against one another.

"I heard what your sisters said about the pumpkins coming alive." Haywood peered at me, his expression suddenly serious. "Maybe it isn't a joke."

"Excuse me?" I said. "What are you talking about?"

My heart started to pound a little faster. Was he about to explain why so many weird things were happening to me on this farm?

"You don't know about this place?" I could barely hear him over the drumming of the rain. He suddenly was speaking in a low voice, just above a whisper.

I shook my head. "What about it?"

He studied me for a long moment. "Maybe you don't want to hear it, Devin. It's kind of a scary story."

"Tell me," I said. "I need to hear it. I need to know what's up with this place."

"Follow me." He led the way to the little shed where I had spent the day. There was just room for the two of us. At least it was out of the rain.

"Guess what used to be here on this land?" Haywood said. He pointed to the pumpkin field. "A graveyard."

I swallowed. "Really?"

"A very old graveyard," he said. "My dad told me it went back to the Civil War."

"Wow," I said. "You mean dead people are buried under this field?"

He nodded. "Yeah. See, that's the problem. This was a graveyard for over a hundred years. Then some farmer came along and decided to plow right over it and start a farm."

My brain was whirring. I didn't quite understand. "You mean he didn't dig up the graveyard first? He didn't move the bodies?"

"No, he didn't," Haywood said softly.

We both stared out at the field for a while. The mist had settled low over the ground. It swirled and curled over the pumpkins *like a floating ghost.*

"He left the dead bodies in the ground," Haywood continued. "And he planted his crops right on top of them."

I swallowed again. My mouth suddenly felt very dry. "So we are walking around over a lot of dead people?" My voice came out tight and shrill.

Haywood nodded. "That's where the stories about this farm got started," he said.

"Stories?"

"Well, some say the dead are very unhappy here. The poor people who are buried in this field don't have gravestones or anything. It makes them angry."

I stared hard at him. I didn't like this story. But I didn't want him to stop.

"Sometimes weird things happen on this farm," he continued. "Frightening things. Things that can't be explained."

"I . . . I know what you're talking about," I stammered.

"They say it's the dead people. They are showing how unhappy they are."

"The dead people . . . ?" I repeated. I felt a shiver run down my back.

"Come with me," Haywood said. "I'll show you something."

I followed him out of the tiny shed. The rain had slowed, but the mist swirled around us in gusts of wind. It was almost like walking inside a cloud.

He led the way along the pumpkin vines till we got to a corner of the field. A mouse scampered over my shoes and disappeared into the shaking leaves.

We stopped. Haywood bent down. He pulled

the green leaves away from a fat vine. "Devin, look here," he said.

He held the leaves to the side so I could see the vine clearly. This was where the vine started. I could see where it sprouted up from the dirt.

"See? The vine goes straight down," Haywood said. "The vine goes straight down into one of the dead people. It's sprouting from a dead body."

"Huh?" A gasp escaped my throat.

"The vines sprout from the corpses down below," Haywood said, still holding the leaves. "And some people say . . . Some people say the angry dead send their spirits . . . their souls . . . through the vines. They send their anger up from their graves . . . through the vines . . . and into these pumpkins."

I gaped at him in silence. Another shiver rolled down my back.

*Was that story totally crazy?*

*Did it make any sense at all?*

I struggled to understand. "You mean, in a way, these pumpkins really *are* alive?" I choked out.

He nodded solemnly. "The pumpkins are alive. Alive with the anger of the dead people they sprout from."

"But — that's *crazy*!" I blurted.

173

Haywood shrugged. "You don't have to believe it if you don't want to."

"But . . . some strange things have happened to me," I said. "Do you think maybe — ?"

"There's more," he said. "Do you want me to tell you the rest?"

I stared hard at him. "I guess. . . ." I turned to the field — and gasped as I saw a pumpkin move. It rolled toward us. Even in the thick mist, I could see it move.

I grabbed Haywood's shoulder. "Did you see that?" I asked. "Did you see that pumpkin move?"

He shook his head. "It's very foggy. Are you sure?"

I kept my eyes on the field. Were all the pumpkins moving now? Were they all rolling on their vines? Moving through the heavy white fog?

"Now I'm not sure," I said. "Can the spirits of the buried people make the pumpkins move?"

"I don't know," Haywood answered. "I'm just telling you the stories I've heard. There's one more. The story of the person they call the Grave-Master."

As he said that word, a burst of wind made the whole field tilt and sway. The fog curled along the vines. The pumpkins were invisible in the mist.

"They say that the angriest dead person of them all rose up through the vines," Haywood continued in a whisper. "His angry spirit traveled through the vines and into a pumpkin. After a while, he learned how to shift his shape."

"I . . . I don't understand," I stammered. "Shift his shape?"

"From inside a pumpkin, he can shift to another shape. Another body. He can be a human or an animal. And then he shifts back into a pumpkin. That way, he cannot be found. He cannot be sent back to where he belongs. His power is strongest on Halloween."

"Uh . . . wow." I had to think about this. This was hard to get my brain around.

"He is called the Grave-Master," Haywood said. "But he can be anywhere his anger takes him. And he wants only one thing. He wants to terrify people and drive them away from —"

Haywood stopped. He didn't finish his sentence. His mouth opened in a startled O.

I followed his gaze. To the field. Into the heavy fog.

And I saw a dark spot through the misty cloud. A black object.

The fog curled away, like a gray-white snake. And the dark object Haywood stared at came into sharper view.

The black cat. Zeus.

Standing stiffly at the edge of the field. Eyes glowing eerily. Trained on us.

Haywood gripped my arm. I could see the fear on his face.

"That c-cat," he stuttered. "How long has he been standing there? Did he hear what we were saying?"

The cat meowed, a sour cry, as if answering the question.

To my surprise, Haywood let the umbrella fall to the ground and took off running, darting into the fog. A few seconds later, he was gone.

Dad was excited at dinner. He kept pounding his fork and knife on the table and saying, "What a day! What an amazing day!"

Mom squeezed his hand. "Take it easy, Allan. Your face is all red."

"I can't take it easy. Did you see all those people? We took in over a thousand dollars today."

"Does that mean I can have a new American Girl doll?" Dale asked.

"Me, too?" Dolly chimed in. "With two sets of outfits?"

Mom and Dad laughed.

"Stop being selfish," Mom scolded. "This money is for the whole family."

"Dale and I are in the family!" Dolly protested.

"What a day!" Dad said for the tenth time. "The rain is already stopping. So tomorrow should be even better. We'll sell every pumpkin — even the scrawny ones. Those vines will be bare."

I pictured the bare vines stretching across the field like long snakes. The thought gave me a shiver.

"You girls were awesome!" Dad said. He took another helping of roasted potatoes from the big bowl and passed it to Mom. "You were the best greeters!"

"Yaaay!" the twins both cheered.

"It was totally fun," Dolly said. "Except when that little dog got lost."

Mom and Dad both blinked. Dad stopped chewing his chicken. "Little dog?"

The girls nodded. "Didn't you see it?" Dale asked. "These people brought their little black dog, and it slipped off its leash?"

"It ran away," Dolly added. "Just ran off and got lost under the pumpkin leaves."

"I missed this drama," Mom said.

"Didn't you hear the people shouting, 'Chewy! Chewy!'?" Dolly said. "That was the dog's name. Chewy."

"What happened?" Dad asked. "Did they find it?"

"Dale found it," Dolly said. "It was right behind us the whole time. It found a piece of pumpkin rind or something, and it was chewing on it."

"Maybe that's why they call him Chewy," I said.

Mom laughed, but no one else did.

"So the story had a happy ending," Dad said. He started eating his chicken leg again.

"And the man gave Dolly and me each a dollar for finding the dog," Dale said, beaming with pride.

"A dollar each? What are you going to do with it?" Mom asked.

"You can't have it. We're saving it to buy Twizzlers in town," Dolly said.

"Good choice," I said. I love Twizzlers.

Dad turned to me. "You did a good job, too, in your little shed. Did you enjoy it?"

"Not really," I said.

He sighed.

"I know, I know. I'm supposed to change my attitude. But I have to tell you something I heard."

I'd been dying to tell Mom and Dad the story Haywood told me about the farm, the graveyard, and the angry dead people. I wasn't sure the dinner table was the right place to tell the story.

But now, here it was, bursting out of me. I really couldn't hold it in any longer.

Dad reached for the string beans. He pointed to my empty plate. "Devin, how come you're not eating?"

"I want to tell you what I heard. About this farm," I said. "Did you know it used to be a graveyard?"

Mom uttered a surprised cry. "Excuse me? A graveyard?"

Dolly squinted across the table at me. "You mean, like, with dead people?"

"Yes," I said. "There was an old graveyard here. Right where the pumpkin fields are."

"That's crazy. Where did you hear that?" Dad demanded.

Before I could answer, Mrs. Barnes came through the kitchen door. She had two bags of groceries in her arms. Dad jumped up to help her carry them to the kitchen counter.

"Did this farm used to be a graveyard?" he asked her.

Mrs. Barnes blinked a few times. She smoothed down the front of her flannel shirt. "You hear a lot of stories," she said. "You can't believe them all, you know."

"Haywood told it to me," I said.

She laughed. "Like I said, you can't believe every story. That boy of mine has a strange and wonderful mind. He's a good boy. But he lives in some kind of fantasy world. Not the world we know."

Dad sat back down at the big kitchen table. Mrs. Barnes reached into a bag and started putting away groceries.

"Go on," Mom said. "What's the rest of the story? Is it too scary for the girls?"

"Nothing scares us!" Dolly declared.

I glanced around the table. They were all staring at me. I knew none of them would believe me.

Mrs. Barnes was right. It had to be some kind of crazy fantasy story.

Dead people don't send their anger up through pumpkin vines. Pumpkins aren't alive with the spirits of people who died a hundred years ago. And no one can rise up from the dead and take the shape of . . .

. . . of a black cat?

I lowered my eyes to the floor. Sure enough, Zeus stood right beside my chair. The cat was gazing up at me, as if waiting for me to finish my story.

No. No way. The whole thing was crazy.

But then, why had Haywood looked so

181

frightened when he saw Zeus watching us from the field? Why did he run away like that?

Was he just putting on an act?

"I'll tell you the whole thing later," I said. "It's just a crazy story."

I had no idea the story was about to get a *lot* crazier.

After dinner, I watched a movie on TV with the girls. It was a comedy about a boy who switches bodies with his father. It was totally embarrassing, but the twins thought it was a riot.

The farmhouse had no wireless or Internet connection. So my laptop was useless. If my friends were trying to reach me online, too bad.

"You guys should get to bed," Mom said. "Tomorrow is a big day. Halloween."

The twins scurried off to their room. I wasn't feeling tired, but I went to my room and read for an hour or so. I was reading one of these *dystopian* novels. That's a book about when all the cities have been destroyed, and there are only a few survivors struggling to get by.

This book was about these people who find out they're the last family on Earth. They're not too happy about it.

Can you imagine if *my* family was the last family on Earth? Ha. Now *that* would be a *horror* story!

I didn't know how late it was. There was no clock in my room. Just a creaky, hard bed with a smelly quilt on it and a beat-up dresser and nothing else.

But my eyelids felt as heavy as rocks. And I was yawning and yawning. So I figured it was time to go to sleep.

I thought about tomorrow. I hoped Dad would let me work the cash register again. I felt safer in that little shed.

I changed into my pajamas. They were Spider-Man pajamas. My dad's idea of a joke. He knows I'm not into superheroes. At least they were warm.

I clicked off the ceiling light, climbed under the ratty quilt, and pulled it up to my chin. The pillow was soft, but I could feel the feathers inside it on the back of my head.

A glow of silvery moonlight washed into my room from the window facing my bed. The window was open, I realized. The curtains fluttered softly on both sides.

It had stopped raining, but I could still hear the patter of raindrops falling from the trees. The wind through the window felt warm, warmer than during the day.

I gazed at the window, waiting for sleep to creep over me.

Something moved. Something outside.

In the silvery moonlight, I saw shadows at the window. Something rose into view, then slid back down.

Blinking, I sat up straight. And peered through the dim light at the open window.

Again, I saw shadows reflected on the fluttering curtains. Something stretched up . . . straight up. It appeared to coil toward the window.

It was slender and pointed at one end. Not a snake. No. Not a snake. *Too big* to be a snake.

It swung against the side of the window. Then appeared to sway from side to side.

Then it curled onto the window ledge.

And I recognized it. I knew what it was.

I didn't believe it. But I saw it clearly now.

A pumpkin vine.

A single vine sliding over the window ledge into my room.

Yes. Stretching silently toward me.

And as I gaped, frozen in horror, unable to speak, unable to make a sound, I saw a second one. Yes. A second vine. Fatter. Thicker.

It rose up beside the first vine. Coiled around it. The vines curled together. Like shoelaces being tied.

Then they came apart. Thrashing. Whipping each other. Pushing ... pushing into my room.

Pale and gleaming in the moonlight, they slithered over the window ledge — reaching for my bed ... reaching for ME.

I opened my mouth to call for help. But no sound came out.

Besides, my parents' room was at the far end of the hall. They wouldn't hear me.

And they wouldn't believe me. I knew what would happen if I ran down to their room and dragged them back. The vines would be gone.

And Dad would frown at me. And accuse me of making up another story because I didn't want to be on this farm.

No way Mom or Dad would believe this. Who would?

I gripped the edge of the quilt so tightly, my hands ached. Sitting up straight as a board, every muscle tense, I watched the two vines thrash and twist and crawl into my room.

The curtains fluttered harder, as if trying to get away from the intruders. The moonlight made them glow like they were electric.

I forced myself out of bed. The floorboards were cold beneath my bare feet. My whole body shook and shuddered.

*It's like a horror movie. Only it's real. And it's happening to ME.*

Okay. I knew I had to do something. I was all alone here. No one to help me. *Devin O'Bannon Versus the Creeping Vine Creatures.*

Go, Devin! Go, Devin!

I took a deep breath and held it.

Then I dove forward. Dove to the window. I dodged around the two vines curling through the air. Dodged around them, my heart doing flip-flops in my chest.

Still holding my breath, I lurched to the window. I raised both hands to the top of the frame — and I *slammed* it shut as hard as I could.

Slammed it down onto the vines. Slammed it. Slammed it on them.

They groaned. A sick, ugly sound. Like a burp from deep in a fat belly.

I heard them groan as the wooden window frame sliced right through them. *Slissssh.*

Yes!

It sliced through the vines. Cut them. Cut them off.

The vine ends thudded to my bedroom floor. A foot long. No. Maybe longer. They dropped heavily to the floor and didn't move.

Finally, I let out a long whoosh of air and breathed again. I stared down at the thick lumps at my feet. And I took breath after breath.

A hard tapping on the window glass made me raise my eyes.

And to my horror, I saw the two cut vines, dark liquid trickling from their open ends. The vines, cut off at the ends, oozed a thick liquid. *Like blood.*

I gasped as they bumped up against the glass. Battered the glass, then pulled back — and batted the window again. Again.

*They won't stop until they break in.*

"Noooo!" I let out a scream. I dove to the window.

"Go away! Now! Go away!" I shrieked. I pounded the window glass with both fists. "Go away! Go! Go!"

I stood there in a terrified panic, pounding and screaming at the thrashing vines on the other side of the window. "Get away from here! Get away!"

I didn't stop screaming until a crash behind me made me nearly jump out of my skin. I wheeled around. "No! Go away!" I cried.

It took me a few seconds to realize the crash had been my bedroom door swinging open. My dad burst in, tying the belt of his bathrobe as he entered.

He squinted through the darkness at me. "Devin? What's going on? I heard you screaming. Why are you at the window?"

"Dad, it — it's the vines!" I stammered. "Come here. Quick. Look." I pointed frantically out the window. "The vines —"

He followed my gaze. Of course, the window was empty now. The glass reflected the pale white moonlight.

Nothing there.

"Vines?" Dad asked, narrowing his eyes at me. "Devin, were you having another nightmare?"

"No, Dad," I started. "I haven't been asleep. The vines were crawling into my room. I was so frightened. I —"

Dad gazed down at the floor beneath the window. He clicked on the ceiling light. Then he moved quickly to the window, his bare feet thudding on the floor.

He bent down and picked up the two stubs of vine. The ends I had sliced off. He held them up and examined them.

"See?" I cried. "Proof, Dad. The vines were climbing into my window. See? I'm telling the truth."

Dad turned to me, holding a vine stub in each hand. "How did these get here, Devin?"

"I cut them off. I cut them with the window."

"But how did they get in your room? Are your sisters playing one of their tricks on you?"

"No, Dad. No trick. Don't you believe me? There's proof. The two vines, they were moving, climbing in through the window."

"But, Devin," Dad said. "Come here."

I walked over to the window. He put his hands on my shoulders. "Look out there." He turned me to the window. "Look down on the grass. It's nearly as bright as day in the moonlight. Do you see any vines?"

I squinted down into the backyard. No vines.

I saw a shovel lying in the grass. Near the garage, one of the twins' bikes lay on its side. And I saw the cat. . . .

Zeus sitting up straight on his haunches, his face tilted toward my window. The black cat, surrounded by a pool of silver moonlight, green eyes glowing. Watching the window. Watching me stare down at him.

"Dad," I whispered, "there's something weird about that cat."

Dad pressed his face against the glass and peered down. "Yes, you're right. That cat never sleeps. It's a very weird cat."

"Dad, you don't believe that the soul of a dead person can rise up and take the shape of something else . . . I mean, like a cat, for instance? You don't believe that a human can inhabit a cat?"

He laughed and shook his head. "Where do you come up with these crazy stories, Devin? Really. Sometimes I think you're from another planet."

He dropped the two vine stubs onto the window ledge. Then he led me back to my bed.

"So I guess you don't believe me about the vines trying to climb through my window?"

"Of course not," he said. He pulled down the quilt and waited for me to climb under it. "Next thing, you'll say that a bunch of pumpkins rolled across the field, bounced up, and jumped on you."

"Funny," I muttered.

"Go to sleep, okay?" He tucked the quilt under my chin. Then he patted my cheeks the way he always does. "Everything will be fine, Devin. We're doing great. Try to enjoy it."

*Enjoy it?*

He shut off the light and made his way out of my room.

*I'm on my own,* I realized.

*I'm the only one who knows there's something terribly frightening about this farm.*

*I'm the only one who can do something about it.*

I had to talk to Haywood. He was the only other person who would believe what was happening here. Maybe he could help.

Haywood knew about the Grave-Master. And he was afraid of Zeus. So he probably figured out that Zeus held the angry spirit inside him. The black cat was the Grave-Master.

Zeus was behind all the terrifying things that were happening. The cat was always there, watching everything.

He controlled the angry energy of the pumpkin

field. He controlled the vines, the pumpkins, everything.

And what did he want? To scare us away so the dead could sleep in peace?

Did that mean he had something horrifying planned for tomorrow — Halloween?

I heard a soft thump. Then another.

I sat up. I gazed at the windowsill. Empty.

I lowered my eyes to the floor. And uttered a soft cry.

The two vine stubs. As I stared in disbelief, they were inching their way toward my bed.

Inching their way, like big worms. Moving silently and steadily across the room toward me.

"Noooo!" An angry wail burst from my throat.

I shoved the quilt aside and leaped to the floor. Without thinking I ran up to the crawling vine stubs.

And I began jumping up and down on them with my bare feet.

"Die! Die! Die!" I shrieked at the top of my lungs.

The vines squished and splattered under my feet. They felt hot and wet on my soles.

"Die! Die! Die!"

I screamed and stomped on them. Stomped on them until they were a pulpy mush that stuck to the soles of my feet.

Gasping for breath, I gazed down at the green-yellow mess on my bedroom floor.

I bent over, spread my hands over my knees, and struggled to catch my breath.

I had defeated them for today.

But what about tomorrow?

# 15

"Haywood, I've got to talk to you." I cornered him by the cash register shed.

Mom was setting up her table of pumpkin pies. The twins were arguing about where they should stand to greet people when the farm opened. Dad was inspecting the field, making sure there were enough pumpkins for people to pick.

It was a cloudy morning. The ground was crunchy and hard from a heavy frost the night before. I could see my breath steam in front of me.

"It's getting serious," I told Haywood. "I really need help."

He glanced around, his eyes following my dad. "I can't talk right now. I'm doing the cash register today. I don't want to get in trouble."

"I begged my dad to let me work the cash register," I said. "I really don't want to be in the field today. The vines . . ."

"Devin — come give me a hand!" Dad shouted. I saw him waving me over to him.

I took a deep breath. I thought about those vines last night. How could I *not* think about them?

"Devin — get a move on!" Dad shouted.

"Coming!" I started to jog into the field. I jumped over a thick vine. My legs brushed fat leaves out of my way as I ran.

Something caught my eye at the edge of the field. The black cat. Zeus watching, as always.

Watching . . . and waiting?

I felt a shiver run down my back. That cat was evil. Would I ever be able to prove it?

"Dad, are you sure I can't work in the shed today?" I asked.

"I'm sure," he said. "It's Haywood's turn. Help with those pumpkins, will you? Pull them out from under the leaves so people can see them."

"Uh . . . okay," I muttered.

"It's Halloween, in case you forgot," Dad said. "Our big day. I need you to be a big help today, Devin."

"No problem," I muttered, my eyes on the cat.

Dad hurried to another row of pumpkins. I bent down and grabbed a pumpkin half hidden by thick leaves. The pumpkin felt cold, as if it had been left in the freezer overnight.

I shivered again as a blast of cold air shook the leaves all around.

And I heard a whisper. A soft whisper. Not the wind. Definitely not the wind.

I stood up and listened. The fat green leaves trembled and shook. And whispered.

Whispered my name.

I wasn't imagining it. I heard my name so clearly. Whispered under the slapping and clapping of the leaves on the vines.

"*Devvvvvvvvvvin* . . . *Devvvvvvvin* . . ."

"Who's whispering?" I cried. "Who is here?"

"*Devvvvvvvvvvin* . . . *Devvvvvvvin* . . ."

Breathy voices all around me. Surrounding me. Whispered voices so clear, carried on the wind, rising over the clap of the leaves.

"Dad — do you hear that?" I shouted. "Do you hear the whispering? Dad?"

He was too far away. He didn't turn around.

And I stood there, frozen in terror. Surrounded by the long, ugly vines and the slapping leaves and the cold, cold pumpkins. And listened . . .

"*Devvvvvvvvvvin . . . Devvvvvvin . . .*"

# 16

Cars pulled into the parking lot. Families piled out, eager to find their last-minute pumpkins.

I had no choice. I had to ignore the whispers and help our customers. We had so many customers, I barely had time to breathe.

I glimpsed Mom's table. She had sold all the little pumpkins with painted faces. And all the pumpkin pies were gone. She had only a few jars of pumpkin butter left.

The twins were having a great time, talking to everyone who arrived, greeting them and making them laugh.

Dad was guiding families along the vines, leading them to the best pumpkins that were left.

Everyone was having a good time. Except me. No way I could relax. Every muscle in my body was tensed.

I was waiting to see what would happen next. The whispers had stopped. Did that mean the angry vines and pumpkins were getting ready to spring their next horror?

As I walked through the field, carrying pumpkins for customers, I thought of the dead people down below my feet. I was sure they could hear or feel the footsteps of all the people walking over their graves.

And I knew it had to make them even angrier.

The vines sprouted from the old corpses down there. The dead sent their anger up through the vines ... into the cold, cold pumpkins I was carrying.

"Can you help me take this to my car?" It was a young woman in a red down coat and a wool cap with earflaps. She pointed to a large pumpkin half hidden by leaves.

"No problem," I said. I hoisted the pumpkin off the ground in both hands and twisted it free from the vine. It weighed a ton. I'm only twelve and I'm not the most athletic guy around.

But it was my job. So I wrapped my hands around the big thing and . . .

. . . And to my shock, the hard, cold rind suddenly changed. I mean, it turned soft. As I held it, the whole thing turned soft as mashed potatoes.

And my hands plunged right into the pumpkin.

Yes. They sank right into the middle of the soft, pulpy pumpkin.

The woman uttered a cry. "What did you do? Why did you do that to my pumpkin?"

"I — I didn't —" I started.

Both of my hands were buried in the pumpkin. I tried to slide them out. But they wouldn't budge.

"Hey, I'm stuck!" I cried.

The woman's face was twisted in confusion. "Are you crazy? Why are you doing that?"

"No. I — I'm really stuck," I stammered. "I can't get my hands out. This pumpkin — it's like glue!"

She shook her head. Her earflaps flopped around. "You're joking, right?"

My dad came hurrying over. "What's the problem here?" His eyes stopped on the pumpkin in my hands. "Put that pumpkin down, Devin," he said. "Why did you crush it like that?"

He slid the pumpkin off me. It left thick orange glop up and down the sleeves of my denim jacket.

He turned to the woman. "Do you see another pumpkin you would like?"

The woman pointed to another big pumpkin. "I guess that one."

"Devin will be happy to carry it for you," Dad said. He motioned me toward the pumpkin.

My sleeves smelled horrible. The pumpkin goo was wet and sticky.

I ignored it and bent down. I twisted the pumpkin off the vine. Then I raised it to my chest.

"Ohhhh." I uttered a groan as the pumpkin turned soft and my hands sank right into its middle.

Dad's face turned red and his eyes started to blink a lot, which is what he does when he's *very* angry. "Devin." He said my name through clenched teeth. "I think your workday is over. Go to the house."

"Dad, I —" I started to argue. But no way I could convince him this pumpkin thing wasn't my fault.

"Sorry," I muttered.

The woman looked very embarrassed. My dad's face was still red as a tomato. I turned and trudged out of the pumpkin field.

My jacket was covered in pumpkin goo. And as I walked, head down, the whispers started up again. Whispers up and down the field . . .

"*Devvvvvin . . . Devvvvvvin . . .*"

My whole body shuddered. In my whole life, I'd never felt so frightened. Or so alone.

I saw Haywood ringing the cash register, handing a man some change. I ran over to the shed. My head was ringing with the soft whispers.

I barged right up to him. "You have to help me. They're out to get me."

He squinted at me. "Who? Who's out to get you?"

"I — I don't know," I stammered. "The pumpkins. The vines. Everything. Can you help me? You know all about this farm. Haywood, is there anything you can do?"

He glanced down. I saw what he was gazing at. Zeus. The black cat, watching us from the front of the shed.

"No. I don't think so," Haywood said, eyes on the cat. "I don't think I can help you, Devin. Sorry."

"You have to," I insisted. I grabbed the front of his parka. I held on to it tight. "You've got to help me. Meet me after dinner. So we can talk."

He still kept his gaze on the black cat. "I . . . don't think so," he said.

"You have to come," I insisted, gripping his coat. "After dinner. Come to the farmhouse. I'll meet you in the back. Please."

The whispers grew louder. I thought I saw pumpkins rolling in the field. Rolling toward me.

*"Devvvvvin . . . Devvvvvvin . . ."* The whispers rang in my ears.

# 17

I couldn't eat my dinner. Spaghetti and meat-balls. The meatballs looked like little round pumpkins to me. And the spaghetti was the crawling, curling vines.

When Mrs. Barnes brought out a pumpkin pie for dessert, I nearly puked my guts out all over the dinner table.

No one noticed. Everyone was too happy and excited to notice me.

They were all talking at once and laughing and joking. Dad was in the *best* mood. His pump-kin-farm idea had worked out for him *big-time.*

I was the only quiet person at the table. I was the only one there who knew of the horror right beyond our backyard.

A few hours after dinner, I went outside to wait for Haywood. It was a cool, breezy night. The full moon floated low in the sky.

I paced back and forth along the back of the house. My hands were cold and sweaty. I kept them jammed into my jeans pockets as I walked. Back and forth. Back and forth.

Where was he? *Where?*

And then I saw the vines. Several vines lifting themselves out of the field. Creeping like snakes over the grass toward the house.

The moonlight was so bright, I could see every line and groove and track on the thick vines as they slithered toward me.

They curled over one another, tangling and untangling. And sliding quickly forward. Gleaming in the bright moonlight.

*Where is Haywood? I need him. Where IS he?*

Gaping in horror at the approaching vines, I saw something move in the dirt. In the dirt where the backyard ended and the pumpkin field began, I saw something rise up.

Was it some kind of small animal? No.

A hand. Squinting into the moonlight, I realized

I was staring at a human hand. Poking up from the dirt.

I could see it so clearly. I watched the fingers move, as if testing themselves. Then the dirt parted and the hand rose higher into the night air.

I saw a slender arm. A coat sleeve. And then a second hand shot up from under the ground. Two arms.

And a head. A head rose up from the dirt. Then . . . shoulders.

The hands pushed down on the grass. And a figure climbed out from under the ground. . . . Under the ground!

From a *grave*?

Someone climbing out from a grave?

I couldn't move. I couldn't breathe.

I watched him rub dirt off his face. Then he brushed off the front of his coat. The legs of his jeans.

He staggered forward. Stepped into a pool of light. And I recognized him.

Haywood.

# 18

My body quivered with horror. I stared at the figure in the moonlight until my eyes blurred.

Was Haywood *dead*? Was he one of the corpses buried under the pumpkin field?

I hate zombie movies. I think they're really dumb. But here I was, *living* in one.

And suddenly I remembered. I remembered asking Haywood where he lived. When I asked, he pointed to the pumpkin field. He said he lived there with his dad and a lot of other people.

And now here he came, brushing off the dirt from his grave and walking across the backyard, past the slithering vines. Walking toward the house because I had invited him. I had begged him to come tonight. To help me.

But he wasn't coming to help me. What was he planning?

I tried to hide. Too late to run. I pressed myself into the darkness of the back wall. I held my breath. My heart beat so hard, my chest ached.

"Devin? I can see you," Haywood said. "Are you hiding there? I've come to help you."

I didn't move from the wall. "No, th-thanks," I stuttered. "I don't need your help anymore. Thanks anyway."

"Yes, you do," he said. "You need my help."

"NO!" I uttered. Actually, I screamed the word. I couldn't hide my panic.

"I came to help you," he repeated. "Because you're my friend. I know all about this farm, Devin. I know how to keep people safe."

He stepped into the shadows. I hugged myself to stop trembling. "I . . . I'm going inside now," I said. "I'm tired from carrying all those pump-kins today."

"Let me come in with you," he whispered. "I have some things to tell you. Important things, Devin."

"No. Really. I'm too tired. Maybe tomorrow?"

I couldn't see his face. The shadows at the back of the house were too deep.

"It's Halloween night," he said. "There are things I need to tell you. To keep you safe on this farm."

My brain was spinning. How could I escape him?

I'd seen him climb up from under the ground. I knew he had to be some kind of zombie.

He moved closer. I heard him chuckle. "Devin, you look so frightened."

"Huh? Me? No way," I protested. But my trembling voice gave me away.

"Why are you shaking?" he demanded.

"It's . . . cold out here," I said.

His next words sent a shock wave down my whole body. *"It's colder in the grave, Devin."*

He grabbed my wrist — and jerked me forward.

I nearly fell over.

His hand tightened around my wrist. It felt like a cold metal clamp.

I tried to pull free. But he was incredibly strong.

"Colder in the grave," he repeated.

"Let go of me! Wh-what do you want?" My voice came out high and shrill.

"I want you to come with me," he said softly. His bone-hard fingers dug into the skin on my wrist. "I want you to come see my grave."

"No! Let go! Let go!"

Panic shot through my body. I twisted and squirmed. "Let *go*!"

But I wasn't strong enough to break his hold.

He turned and started to pull me across the wet grass. I struggled against him, but he was just too powerful.

"Stop!" I cried. "I don't want to see your grave! Let me go!"

He turned. His eyes were glassy. Empty. Like doll's eyes. "It doesn't hurt," he said in a whisper.

"Doesn't hurt? *What* doesn't hurt?" I cried.

"It doesn't hurt to die, Devin. You'll see."

"No! Please!"

He began pulling me again, forcing me over the grass toward the field. Gripping me with his steel-like hand. Pulling with horrifying strength.

*He's going to pull me into his grave.*

I twisted back toward the house. I tried to shout for my parents. But the windows were all shut against the cold. The lights were all out. Everyone was asleep.

No way they could hear my feeble cries.

Haywood pulled me over the vines, which were twisting together, curling, uncurling. As I passed by, they reached up as if to grab me. But he tugged me out of their reach.

*I'm doomed.*

I realized no one could save me. And he was too strong for me to save myself.

I opened my mouth to shout again. But there was no one around. No one who could help me.

And then my eyes fell on a dark figure at the edge of the field. And I realized I had one tiny hope left.

"Zeus!" I shouted. "Zeus — you're the Grave-Master. You can help me!"

The cat tilted his head at my words. His green eyes caught the moonlight and appeared to glow.

"Zeus! I know who you really are! I know you are in control of everyone here. Zeus — please. Help me. Stop Haywood. Stop him!"

The cat lowered his head. He took a step toward us. Then another.

Haywood turned to face him.

"Yes!" I cried. "Come stop him! You are the Grave-Master! You can do it! Help me! Help me, Zeus."

The cat took another step toward us into the leafy field. He raised his head, and his eyes glowed brightly at Haywood.

"Get him, Zeus!" I screamed.

I held my breath as the cat eyed Haywood.

The fat pumpkin leaves rustled all around us, shifting and bending in the cold October wind. Even the moonlight felt cold on my face as I stared . . . stared waiting for the cat to make his move.

Haywood tightened his grip on my arm.

The cat tilted his head and meowed. A soft mew.

Haywood tossed back his head and laughed. He reached down with his free hand and tickled the cat under his chin.

Zeus mewed again.

Haywood grinned at me. "He's just a cat, Devin. That's all."

My mouth dropped open. "You mean — ?"

"I mean, I tricked you," Haywood said. "To throw you off the track. I made you think the cat was the Grave-Master, and you believed it — didn't you. So sorry. I can see how disappointed you are. But Zeus is just a cat. A big, lazy cat."

"Noooo," I moaned as Haywood began to pull me again. I tried to dig my shoes into the soft ground. But he was inhumanly strong. I couldn't hold back.

My mind was spinning. But I was so frightened, my thoughts made no sense at all.

"So . . . *you* are the Grave-Master?" I asked him.

He laughed again. "Wrong," he said. "You are wrong about everything, Devin."

He pulled me to a hole in the field. A perfect rectangle dug between the leafy vines.

I peered down. Dark inside. Too dark to see how deep it was.

But I recognized it. It was a grave. It was going to be *my* grave.

Suddenly, a few feet from the open grave, the dirt began to move. Chunks of dirt flew up from the ground. A hand poked up. The hand fumbled until it found a thick vine.

I stared in horror as the fingers wrapped around the vine. I knew what was happening. Another corpse was rising up from its grave.

"Want to meet the Grave-Master?" Haywood said, watching the ground along with me. "Here is the Grave-Master."

We both stared in silence as a second hand appeared. Both hands tugged on the vine till a head poked up from the dirt.

Mrs. Barnes.

Dirt slid and tumbled out of her way as she pulled herself up. After a few seconds, the big woman stood grinning at me. She brushed dirt chunks from her long braids. She held something in one hand.

A pumpkin.

"Well, well. Here we are," she said. "Do you know what night it is, Devin? It's the Night of the Jack-o'-lantern."

She raised the pumpkin higher — and it lit up. Orange flames blazed inside it. And I could see big triangle eyes and a jagged mouth cut in a cruel scowl.

Mrs. Barnes shoved the fiery jack-o'-lantern close to my face.

"It's the Night of the Jack-o'-lantern, Devin. The jack-o'-lantern laughs at death. Are *you* ready to laugh at death?"

"No — please!" I cried, trying to back away. But Haywood held me tightly in place.

"Watch the jack-o'-lantern's grin as you go down below," Mrs. Barnes said, still smiling at me. Her round cheeks were smeared with dirt. She pulled a worm out of her nose and tossed it to the ground.

"But — why me?" I cried in a high, frightened voice. "I don't understand."

"It's easy to explain. My boy Haywood needs a friend," Mrs. Barnes said. "It gets lonely under this field. As lonely as death. Haywood needs someone his own age to spend the long days with."

I stared at her. "Me? A friend?"

"The vines," I said, "attacking my room. The pumpkins . . . the whispers . . . It only happened to me. No one else in my family."

"That's because I chose you," Mrs. Barnes said. "You are Haywood's age. I mean, Haywood was twelve when he died one hundred and twenty years ago. I chose you to be his friend."

"But — but I don't understand —" I didn't know what I was saying. I just thought if I could keep her talking, maybe . . .

"Time to go down," Mrs. Barnes said. She raised the scowling jack-o'-lantern above her head. Then she signaled to Haywood with a nod.

Haywood pushed me to the edge of the grave.

My shoes slipped on the soft dirt. I stared down into the deep black hole.

"Do you want to jump?" Haywood whispered in my ear. "Or do you want me to push you?"

# 20

He grabbed my shoulders from behind. My shoes slid closer to the deep black hole of the grave. One push . . . one push, and I was gone.

I felt his fingers tighten on my shoulders. Ready to shove me down into my grave.

A wild scream rang over the field.

At first, I thought it was *my* scream. It took a few seconds to realize it was from someone else.

I felt Haywood's hands loosen on my shoulders. I stumbled back. We both turned. All three of us stared at the roaring figure running across the field at us.

As this person ran into the moonlight, I saw a bright green costume. A Halloween costume? The hideous scream — like a furious wild beast — roared out from an ugly mask.

The mask was green and creased and rutted. It had huge, sharp fangs poking out of its open mouth. The ears were long and pointed and standing straight up. The eyes were red and wild.

The ground-shaking roar was so angry and loud, I wanted to cover my ears.

I saw the shock on the faces of Haywood and his mother. They froze like silvery statues in the moonlight. The jack-o'-lantern slid from her hands and rolled across the ground.

The bellowing creature ran up to us. Spread its arms wide. Thick gobs of drool fell from the open snout.

Turned to me. Those red eyes turned to me. Making my whole body shake.

"*It's meeeeee!*" she cried in a raspy animal growl. "*It's meee . . . Luuuuu-Annnn!*"

No. It couldn't be. It couldn't be my friend Lu-Ann.

This was a wild animal. A dangerous creature. A *monster.*

"*It's Luuuu-Annnnn!*" it repeated.

"No — you can't be! You *can't* be!" I cried.

And then it twirled around to face Haywood and Mrs. Barnes. And screamed at them in a bellowing voice that made the trees shake and the ground tremble.

*"GOOOOO AWAAAAAY!"*

The masked creature dove toward them with a terrifying roar. It flung itself on Haywood, tackled him around the waist. The two of them crashed heavily to the dirt.

Eyes wide with shock, Mrs. Barnes stumbled back.

Grunting and groaning, Haywood and the creature wrestled over the ground. The monster let out another roar that shook the trees. Haywood ripped at its face, trying to pull off the mask. But I could see clearly it wasn't a mask. The hideous fanged face *was its face*!

I stood frozen across from Mrs. Barnes, watching helplessly as the battle grew louder and more intense. The monster poked its fingers into Haywood's eyes. Haywood let out a shriek of pain and twisted his face away.

He tugged at the monster's ears. Sent a hard punch into its belly.

Gobs of green drool splatted from the creature's mouth as it rolled on top of Haywood, pounding him with punches, gouging at his eyes.

My mind spun as I watched the horrifying battle. If the creature won, would it fight me, too? I knew that if Haywood won, he would toss me into his grave. But if the monster won . . .

They were both on their feet now, pulling and pushing, struggling to overpower the other, moving closer to the open grave. Closer . . .

And then with a burst of power, Haywood lifted the monster off its feet. He wrapped his arms around its waist and hoisted it high over his head. Then with a loud groan, he turned and held the creature over the grave.

The creature thrashed and kicked. But Haywood was too strong. He raised it higher — and started to heave the monster into the grave.

*What if it really is Lu-Ann?*

I stared at the horrible face.

*How could it be Lu-Ann? But what if it is?*

I shot forward. Lowered my shoulder and plowed hard into Haywood's middle.

He uttered a gasp — and staggered back.

The monster slid from his hands. It screamed as it started to topple into the grave.

I turned and grabbed it. Wrapped my hands around its middle — and swung it to safety on the ground.

With a roar of anger, Haywood came charging at me. I dodged to the side — and he ran

into the open grave. I heard him screaming all the way down. He seemed to fall for a
*long* time.

"Evil!" Mrs. Barnes screamed at the monster.
"Evil!" Then she leaped into the grave and disappeared after her son.

Gasping for breath, I waited for them to return.
But the grave remained silent and dark.

I turned to the creature. It stood with its
hands on the waist of the green costume, breathing noisily, gobs of drool sliding from its fanged
jaws. Its red eyes locked on me. *"You . . .
saved . . . my life."* A raw whisper.

And then its face appeared to loosen. Its whole
head sagged. The red eyes faded. The rows of
pointed teeth drooped. As I gaped in amaze-
ment, it reached up both hands — and tugged off
its head.

A mask after all.

"Lu-Ann!" I shrieked. "It *can't* be!"

She didn't answer. She stared openmouthed at
the hideous mask in her hands. "It came off."
Her voice still a whisper. She shook her head as
if she didn't believe it.

"Devin, you . . . you saved my life," she stammered. "An act of kindness. You thought I was a
monster, didn't you? But you saved my life, anyway. An act of unbelievable kindness."

I moved closer to her. "Lu-Ann, I don't really know what you're talking about."

She crinkled the mask between her hands. "It took an act of kindness to remove the mask. That's what Marcus's dad said. An act of kindness. But not from *me*. Don't you see, Devin? It had to be an act of kindness from *someone else*!"

"Lu-Ann, I still don't understand."

"*Beauty and the Beast*, Devin. *Beauty and the Beast*. I was the Beast."

"I've always known you were a beast," I said. I was starting to feel a little more normal.

She laughed. Then she tossed the mask across the field and began dancing up and down. "I'm free! I'm okay! I'm free! I'm me again! Devin, I'm *me*!"

Lu-Ann pumped her fists above her head. Then she dove forward and hugged me.

"The mask stuck to my face. It turned me evil. I ran and ran," she said. "I didn't know where to go. And then I remembered your farm was here."

"You're okay," I said. "Me, too. We're *both* okay."

She tossed back her head and laughed again. "Happy Halloween, Devin."

"Happy Halloween," I said. "By the way, how was Polly's party?"

# EPILOGUE:

# POLLY'S HOUSE

# THE NEXT DAY

Polly stared down the attic stairs at the line of kids. "Okay, everyone. Keep to the right," she called. "Have your money ready."

Kids laughed and chatted excitedly. One boy near the end of the line made ghost sounds. "*Owoooooo.*" That made more kids laugh.

Polly watched their faces. She could see that they were excited and tense.

"Okay. One at a time," she said. "If you get frightened, just turn around and go back downstairs."

She turned from the stairway to go stand in front of the closet. But Marcus and Brad hurried up behind her. "Polly? What's up with this?" Marcus asked.

"Did you hear about Lu-Ann?" Brad asked. "She ended up at Devin's pumpkin farm last night."

Polly shook her head. "I didn't know that. But, wow. Thanks to Lu-Ann, my party is the hit of the year. Everyone is talking about it."

"But . . . what are they saying?" Marcus asked. "Your party was a total *disaster*."

"Are you kidding? My party was *not* a disaster, Marcus. It was the scariest Halloween party in the history of Dayton, Ohio."

Marcus and Brad both sighed.

"When can we start? We want to see the ghost!" a boy shouted from the stairway.

"Ghost! Ghost! Ghost!" kids started to chant. Their voices echoed up the attic stairs.

"What are you doing?" Brad demanded. "Why are all these kids lined up?"

Polly tossed back her hair. "They want to see the ghost in the closet. Lu-Ann wrecked him last night. But he put himself back together. He's totally terrifying. Everyone wants to get a good look at him."

"You — you mean you're charging admission?" Brad stammered.

"Five dollars," Polly said. "Five dollars per person to see a real ghost."

"But, Polly —" Marcus tried to protest.

Polly pushed him toward the stairs. "Go get in line, guys. You can't stand here. You're in the way. It's time to get started."

Shaking their heads, Brad and Marcus started to the stairs.

But Polly called to them. "Hey, check this out. Look what I found." She held up a dark blue mask.

The two boys squinted at it. "That looks a little bit like the mask Lu-Ann wore last night. Where'd you find it?"

Polly pointed to the open trunk on the floor. "I found it in that trunk. Isn't it sick looking? It looks a *lot* like Lu-Ann's mask. I'm going to put it on now."

"You're *what*?" Marcus cried.

"I'm going to wear it to surprise the kids in line. You know. Make the whole experience creepier."

"You shouldn't —" Marcus started. But Polly waved the two boys away. "Do you have five dollars? Go get in line."

"We've already seen the ghost. For *free*," Marcus said. He followed Brad to the crowded stairway. He turned back as they started down the stairs.

The last thing he saw was Polly pulling on the ugly blue mask.